ANTHONY SILMAN

MAX BOMBER REVENGE

This edition first published in paperback by
Michael Terence Publishing in 2023
www.mtp.agency

Copyright © 2023 Anthony Silman

Anthony Silman has asserted the right to be identified as
the author of this work in accordance with the
Copyright, Designs and Patents Act 1988

ISBN 9781800944954

No part of this publication may be reproduced, stored
in a retrieval system, or transmitted, in any form or
by any means, electronic, mechanical, photocopying,
recording or otherwise, without the prior
permission of the publisher

Cover images
Copyright © Ragged Stone
www.123rf.com

Cover design
Copyright © 2023 Michael Terence Publishing

Michael Terence
Publishing

1

Gary's mother spoke to him. Of course, she did, she was, after all, his mother, but she couldn't hide the anguish seared into her brow. Her eyes, which once scintillated with pride, were now subdued with disappointment. She had hope, all she had was hope, and she clung to it forlornly.

"It's ok, mum," chirped Gary with theatrical positivity, "it'll work this time. I'm so committed, so determined, this time I really want to make it work and I think now, I'm strong enough to beat it."

She smiled her best bright, supportive smile, which didn't quite mask her inner desolation. Gary could see it and feel it, but he couldn't find that last reserve of bravery to acknowledge it in words.

Gary's father was neither sympathetic nor compassionate. Gary senior wanted his son to live up to what he believed to be the worth of his name. He'd had his son christened after him as an expression of lineage continuation. Others thought it more like vanity, especially as Gary senior's dad had been named Eric.

Gary senior, now in his early 70s, had lived a colourful and relatively successful life. His dad, Eric, had been an accountant and imbued his son with a sense of self-reliance and self-responsibility. Gary senior felt he didn't have the personality of an accountant, so with five thousand pounds borrowed from his dad at a commercial rate, he started buying, revitalising, selling, or renting lower-end properties.

He did it well. When Gary senior asked a 'pretty young girl' called Christine, out for a drink, he was a young man with more disposable cash than many of his contemporaries. Christine, who had worked as a counter cashier at the local bank, knew this and consequently found him more attractive than her peers.

Gary senior had an austere upbringing; his dad Eric eschewed luxuries except for a joint of good beef on Sundays. Consequently, Gary senior was also careful with expenditure, the exception being his wedding. "When Gary and Chrissie get married, the whole town will be impressed," he promised his impressionable young fiancée.

Eric was a religious man and a regular worshipper at Worcester Cathedral. He had also provided sound investment advice to the then Bishop, thus Gary and Chrissie were allowed to marry at the Cathedral Church of Christ and the Blessed Mary the Virgin.

A sumptuous reception took place a forty-minute drive away in the limo-de-choix of the time, a long-wheelbase Jaguar, also known to be hired by a famous Birmingham rocker. The imitation renaissance architecture of the gallic Chateau-style hotel gave a satisfyingly indulgent impression, thought Eric. He had given his son an extra five hundred pounds to spend on adding sophisticated elegance to the day. Gary and Chrissie put the donation to good use; booze, lots of it and all very good quality. They toasted themselves several times with Veuve Clicquot, and when the pleasantly sozzled guests became absorbed in boogie and laughter, the married couple crept away like naughty children.

Gary senior and his Chrissie would remember their wedding night forever, not least because eight months and twenty-five days later, Gary junior made his early bid for existence. Chrissie was just twenty-two when she became a mother. Like most young mothers, she felt terrified and frighteningly unprepared. Gary was ten years older and expressed his pride and delight at having a son with more gusto in the pub than at home. He was not a naturally soft, playful, loving dad and wasn't sure he knew how to be.

Chrissie had two maternal trump cards; innate intelligence and more love for the product of her body than she thought humanly possible. She didn't buckle under the strain of being almost solely responsible for a baby. Gary did little to help but still expected all the domestic services demanded of his wife to continue unabated. Chrissie didn't waver under the pressure of sleeplessness, worry, work and partial isolation, in fact, she thrived on it and, as she became more confident and capable as a mother, she began to resent her husband's presence and interference, rare though such intrusions became.

Gary junior and his mother were each other's worlds. Chrissie tried hard to mother without smothering but was protective and acutely risk-averse, alternating between treating Gary as a fragile work of art one moment and a friend and companion, the next. She talked to him as an adult about day-to-day matters, hence Gary junior could talk before he walked.

Going to school came as a fundamental shock to Gary. He knew little of other children and didn't understand what he was supposed to do or how to act. From the outset, Gary felt himself to be an outsider looking in through a window to a world he didn't understand. He protected himself by believing that he was special and different, just as his mother had always told him.

By senior school, Gary had become accustomed to being bullied, always the last one picked for any team and cast as the form wimp. But, as he developed, his confidence grew. He found his quick wit, ability to express himself in most company, and increasing willingness to prove his non-wimpiness by taking risks his mother would have prohibited, all combined to improve his standing in the school's hierarchy of dominance.

By year twelve, still known as the lower sixth in his traditional school, Gary had established his own fiefdom along with a poor academic record and an arrogant disregard for authority and rules. The scars from all those early years of feeling like an interloper in a world belonging to others, all those lower-form years of being bullied and derided, had left Gary junior with no feelings of affinity for his fellow students, and even less pity when one or other hapless victim fell foul of his fiefdom's regime.

Gary established in-school enterprises ranging from running a book with odds on almost anything where a result could be wagered; selling a lot of alcohol, cigarettes and dope, all sourced via extortion and intimidation; through to a flourishing 'Gary Guarantee' service which sold map-drawing, maths calculations, test answers, re-writing online plagiarism and various other profitable flim-flam temptations.

Most of the lazy and less able students were happy to pay Gary for their selected service, but some thought they could renege. Gary understood the principles of strong-arm coercion and employed the more easily managed school thugs to persuade errant customers to pay up with interest. Expulsion, a sanction unwillingly deployed, became inevitable for Gary, who did all he could to hasten its activation. Persistent dishonesty, violence, usury, a disregard for teachers and shameless conduct, plus an unproven but widely believed accusation of sexual harassment, all combined to hasten Gary's exit from academe. At seventeen, with only a handful of Cs and Fs to show, Gary's life faltered. His income ceased the moment he left school, and the prospect of further education didn't enter his thinking.

Chrissie was thrilled to have her baby back at home full-time. The school's head had summoned Gary Snr and Chrissie for an expulsion hearing, but neither attended. Chrissie knew her son was a bit of a rebel and put his expulsion down to his admirable individualism and creative, if perhaps Quixotic, character. She felt convinced that the school had targeted him due to his charismatic and distinctive nature and blamed him for all the wrongs they were unable to right other than by victimising her boy. School had taught Gary Jnr much about survival. Unusually, for a young man devoid of empathy, Gary had an adept chameleon-like quality. He had learned to fit in. He no longer felt like an outsider; his honed and proficient acting skills made him anyone that everyone else wanted him to be.

Back at home, dependent on his mother's love and his father's largesse, Gary Jnr knew the score. To his mum, he was sensitive, kind and considerate. But for his father, he was the tough go-getter, the ambitious and aspirational young follower with fire in his belly and a remarkable life to achieve.

Chrissie bought him his first car, and Gary Snr bought him a fully loaded laptop so his son could continue his studies and follow a work-from-home degree course in Psychology with the University of Wolverhampton. Gary Snr's IT manager had bought the laptop for a now-defunct project. As unused surplus, it presented an inexpensive opportunity for Dad to show his son how generous he could be.

Understanding the value of props to good acting, Gary Jnr applied to, and was accepted by, the University and began his remote-learning course. To his mother's pleasure and his father's surprise, he devoted at least three hours a day to his labours. There was little else to do anyway, and, to his amazement and relief, he found he enjoyed the subject, especially his introduction to the effects of drugs on criminal behaviour and extreme violence.

Over the years that Gary Jnr had been at school, his parents settled into an unplanned, sometimes unwanted life of suburban socialising, which included provincial pastimes such as golf and tennis and acquiring privilege tickets for major events. Gary Snr had been a keen socialiser from his early days when he learned that friends in useful places were valuable indeed. When they were first married, he and Chrissie held parties with more and more sought-after invitations as their reputation for lavish, free-flowing hospitality spread.

When Eric died, he left his son, Gary Snr, with a painful inheritance tax bill, the result of an accountant's imprudence. Its burden was eased by a large amount of residual money, enabling Chrissie and Gary to move into an enviable house with enviable grounds and drive enviable cars; their lot was perceived as a happy one. As Gary Snr's success grew and his affluence swelled, his home life shrivelled. His adoration for the beautiful young Chrissie diminished, his delight at being a dad had been short-lived anyway, and boredom with the mundanity of home life oppressed him more every day.

Gary Snr knew the right medicine for his condition of domestic lassitude, and he could easily afford it. He became everyone's best friend, buying the drinks anywhere, everywhere and frequently. He didn't care if the friendships were shallow, greedy, opportunistic or fake; he craved escapism, the euphoria of booze and its associated bonhomie. Popular, funny and wealthy, Gary Snr became highly covetable to many dispossessed wives, seeking a thrill or, even better, an escape. When sober, Gary Snr was indifferent to rapacious approaches, but, in the grips of drink, he was a susceptible quarry. To him, drunken flirting and fondling was a game; to Chrissie, it was an abhorrent betrayal and an attack on her allure and attractiveness. After Gary Jnr's birth, she had regained her slim elegance in just weeks and prided herself on being the trimmest young mum in town. As her husband's interest in her subsided, her interest in other men grew.

Gary Snr and Chrissie subsequently spent much time accusing each other of infidelity but continued to drift along together in their emotionally detached relationship. They displayed affection for each other at their parties and maintained a social union whenever together; they took little notice of any scandalous tittle-tattle, believing themselves to be as special and different as their son. Meanwhile, Gary Jnr watched and approved; disguising one's true feelings was a worthy and admirable skill, in his opinion. He was also aware of the coercion and mild blackmail opportunities that his parents' peccadillos presented.

Few parents hold parties to celebrate their child's expulsion, but Gary and Chrissie did. To them, it was their prodigy's rite of passage to shrug off the confines of school and evolve into the estimable, high-achieving son of his affluential parents. Gary Jnr loved the party; it reminded him of his very first drink, a sherry at one of his mother's morning 'girls' gatherings'. Since then, he had become an enthusiastic daily drinker to the point of needing what he termed a little heart-starter most mornings. Both his parents had noticed his fondness for the bottle but were not worried; it was the sign of a good chap, and he knew enough about booze to manage it. On the night of his party, Gary Jnr passed out and concussed himself. He could remember nothing the next day as he nursed his bruises and sipped an almost transparent Bloody Mary.

2

"Mr and Mrs Rackham!" giggled Jo Rackham, nee Hadge. "I'll never get used to it, I mean, me a missus again. After Charles, I swore I'd never marry again. You're a complete shit Dan Rackham; look what you've done to me." She waved her wedding ring at her husband.

"Well, Mrs Rackham, I've said it before and I'll say it again, that's what you get for playing footsie with a client."

Jo and Dan met when she was an event organiser and Dan her customer as Chief Operating Officer of the technology security company Onetelcall. They had been happily involved in a lazy, loving relationship when Jo was attacked by an Olderbury drug dealer called Sniff Taylor. He had viciously, violently and potentially lethally attacked her on her doorstep, resulting, to her astonishment, in her being charged and tried for GBH with intent, inflicting on her a long period of harrowing, nerve-shredding anxiety and fear.

After she had been completely exonerated in a three-day-long, angst-ridden trial, Dan discovered that his old friend and boss, Spray Wilson, CEO of Onetelcall at its HQ in Ohio, had been responsible for pushing drugs through the company's European premises. One of Dan's recruits, Max Golby, had admitted to being a part of the drug trafficking operation but, after his revelation, had worked with Dan to trap the odious Sniff in a sophisticated social media trap.

As a result of Sniff's subsequent conviction and imprisonment, the entire drug business, with its roots in Ohio and Mexico, imploded. Spray Wilson had gone into hiding with his Mexican girlfriend. Dan had become a significant shareholder and CEO of Onetelcall with a penitent and reformed Max as his indispensable wingman. Before fleeing, Spray Wilson had ceded his Ohio property and a proportion of his shares to Dan with the intention that the company's HQ would remain in the US. Dan had different ideas. He kept the manufacturing plant in Cleveland and administration offices in Medina but made Olderbury the new worldwide HQ with regional offices in Dordrecht and Strasbourg.

After their wedding, where Max had been the last-minute best man due to Spray's sudden disappearance, Dan and Jo put the trauma of the attack, threat and danger from drug-running villains behind them with a languorous, lustful, indulgent honeymoon in Corsica.

"My lovely girl, we can go anywhere in the world you want," said the in-love Dan, willing to do anything for his bride, "but why Corsica?"

"Because, hubby-chap, it is beautiful, still relatively unspoiled and untouristy, refreshingly unpretentious, and I love it, good enough for you?"

It was everything Jo promised and much more. They stayed in a small, luxurious hotel in Porto Vecchio, and rented an Audi R8 Spyder from the island's prestige car hire company.

"A ridiculous, indulgent boy's toy," commented Jo, "am I not enough to play with?"

They got sun-burned scalps driving their 200 mph supercar at about 40 mph around the lanes and through the mountains. They ate divine Franco-Italian and uniquely Corsican food. They spent idle afternoons sipping pastis, seated at a pavement table overlooking the old citadel of Bonifacio and savoured being onlookers of amiable and entertaining Petanque in the evening shade.

Jo's night-time terrors had subsided, and Dan's obsessions with the men who put Jo's life in danger had waned too, not gone entirely but less stark and harsh now. His hatred of Kevin 'Sniff' Taylor, the callous drug dealer and psychopathically violent misogynist, was only slightly mollified by knowing that he was imprisoned at HMP Frankland, known as Monster Mansion because of the violence of its inmates. He couldn't know that the social media campaign he and Max had planted, the deepfake videos and the imposter posts positioning Sniff as a woman-beater, a mother hater, a violent drug pusher and worse, had disgusted even the Frankland Monsters who conjoined as one to make Sniff's life in prison as hellish as they could.

And they could.

Adapted TENs machines inflicted electrical shocks via heavy-duty pads to Sniff's most vulnerable points; chopsticks to the bottoms of his feet, enforced gag vomiting and mask suffocation were just some of the atrocities the Monsters doled out with sadistic pleasure. The inmates ensured that the relief of losing consciousness was denied to Sniff; his only respite came from long terms of protective solitary confinement.

Dan and Jo had sold their flats in Olderbury and bought a joint marital home on a village green just a few miles from the Onetelcall offices. Feeling restored, refreshed and reinvigorated from their Corsican idyl, Dan parked his yellow BMW in his new drive and they felt glad to be home.

"That's it then Jo, back on yer head," said Dan, referring to a pet old joke as they carried their bags and suitcases into their new home. They decided against unpacking in favour of a bottle of bubbly in their new garden, on their new zero-gravity garden chairs, in their new garden-use bubbly glasses.

Dan raised his glass in a toast, "Here's to our new life Jo, you have already made my life immeasurably more wonderful than I could ever expect and I just want it, us, to carpe every diem and make our lives the best, happiest and most glorious they can be. To you most of all and then to us, my girl, bung bloody ho and bottoms up."

"And up yours too, buddy," riposted Jo, slurping intentionally noisily. "You know it, Dan, I am so happy I can't put it into words…" she put her glass on the table, jumped up and planted a sloppy kiss on Dan's champagne-sticky lips. "Does that say it better?" she asked with a mischievous grin.

"Well, it's a start, I suppose, but I'm sure you can explain yourself better than that," Dan put his glass down too, and the new, fortunately very private, back garden was christened.

As the sun set with magnificent red and orange illuminations, Dan and Jo polished off their bottle and nibbled a plate of cheese, sausage rolls, crisps, tomatoes and gherkins.

"It's going jolly well so far, I'd say," said Dan. "This marriage malarky is a damn good thing in my book. I feel, oh, I don't know, I just feel complete and content. I'd like to be able to stop the clock right now and live this moment."

"I know what you mean," said Jo. "We had so much to deal with, so much we didn't expect, so much nobody would expect; surely, we deserve a bit of peace and happiness now?"

"Abso-bloody-lutely, but even so, I still get that Sunday night feeling of apprehension, like I've got double maths at school again in the morning and I haven't done my homework. Sunday evenings always do it to me. The memories seep back and the old hollow feeling seeps in, it's odd. Thing is, it is back to work in the morning; a proper Monday morning after so long on hols, feels a bit off, really. Oh, I know Max will have done a great job, and I can wander back into my office with nothing to worry about but, well, that Sunday evening syndrome still lingers."

"I used to hate Sunday nights too as a kid," she said. "When I was young, we'd have Sunday lunch and a bit of supper later on and Sunday evening was telly and early bed. Awful, at least I thought then it was awful. I remember cycling to school on Monday mornings and catching that first whiff of school corridor disinfectant; it's a smell that lingers as long as your Sunday syndrome. And for a year at least, we really did have double maths first thing on Monday. But that's the difference between us, matey boy, I loved it 'cos I was good at maths, and I always did my homework."

"Girlie swot," quipped Dan as he stood up. "Come on girl, sleepy time if we are to face a new day."

The new day started joyfully with an enthusiastic welcome from Max as Dan and Jo walked together into Onetelcall's Olderbury HQ.

"Boss! Boss-ess! You Two. It's so good to see you both. Here…" Max proffered a tray of good coffee. "None of that machine crap for the returning heroes," he grinned, "only the best-copulated coffee for the world's favourite lovers."

"I think you mean percolated," said Jo with an eyebrow emphasis as she took a cup.

"Thanks, Max," said Dan, "good to see you too, seems like forever ago since our wedding and your star performance as best man, but here we are again, and it's back to work because we've got a lot to do."

"Yeah, well, the company is in great shape at the minute, boss, as I hope you've seen in my reports if you had time to look."

"Wasn't all sun, fun and frolics, Max. I did read every word of your very detailed mails and, yes, it certainly seems to be running well, you've done a good job and so have Karl in Strasbourg and your chum Chloe in Dordrecht. Whatever Spray turned out to be, he put a great team together in Medina and Cleveland; the whole States operation seems to be leaping along from strength to strength."

"It is, boss," agreed Max. "I went over there, as you know, and I have to say I think it's a smoother operation now in the offices and the plant than it was when Spray was in charge."

"So I see, Max. All the numbers look good, and the forecasts are realistic too. Our core business is solid, no two ways about that but, you know, this pandemic has created a veritable swarm of new threats and those, my friend, mean new opportunities."

The Covid pandemic, still a global scourge, had prompted an unprecedented rise in IT crime of all complexions. Systems controlling Identity and Access had been breached in numerous major corporations. Billions of identities had been filched and millions of records fatally compromised. Such crime was rising by some five hundred per cent by the year. Twin hacking attacks from China and Russia threatened to overwhelm the US, notably where ubiquitous Microsoft and SolarWinds systems were employed. Cybercrime had become the second pandemic, and observers were quick to notice that over forty per cent of the world's hackers were in China, just as the original coronavirus Covid-19 strain had been.

Dan understood that these headline cybercrimes and statistics didn't tell the whole story. He believed that the smaller troll and hacker farms dotted around the world, notably Iran, India and Eastern Europe were the cyber-terrorism threats that occupied the IT intelligence boffins the most. While both Russia and China, along with their assorted allies and easily led factional groups, concentrated on doing anything they could to destabilise the West, the maverick cyber gangs put their efforts into fraud, ransomware, cyber-theft and extortion. Whether state-promoted or gang-driven, the targets were common and obvious. Governments, civil services, big companies, small companies, online commerce, pressure groups, news sources, in fact, anywhere disruption, dislocation, discord and disharmony could be wreaked.

The large-scale corporate attacks defocussed the effect of insidious manipulation of society and societies. Where naivety and gullibility could be exploited by conspiracy or outraged good cause, the hackers and trolls were on it, with significant effect. Many in the West ascribed this activity to Marxism and terrorism, whereas Dan felt that greed and barbaric misanthropy were motives for many cyber incursions and atrocities. He had heard arguments postulating that the West was at war with China, but the majority didn't recognise it. The West's increasing dependency on China for its goods, its investment and financial clout, plus western reliance on Russia for its gas and oil, suggested to some that the war had already been fought and lost and that what the West was experiencing from Covid onwards was a gradual subjugation. Whereas wars had once been fought with tanks, aeroplanes, ships and missiles, the weapons in this putative battle were more mundane, mainly social media and email.

In devising and delivering a deeply deserved comeuppance to Sniff Taylor, Dan and Max had harnessed the potential for malfeasance that email and social media offered in profusion. In so doing, they had learned much about the dark arts from the dark web, about trolling and digital dissimulation and Onetelcall's advanced technological R&D had given them a big advantage.

During their honeymoon, Dan and Jo talked about their fears for the future. The conversations began with children; to have or not to have. Even as they spoke, both Dan and Jo knew that they were creating a very different embryo, one of action against the marauding hordes of hackers and trolls. When Dan had been a customer of Jo's specialist event services, she had introduced him to the CyBOK experts at the National Cyber Security Centre and some of the big brains at the NCSC's MOD facility. In America, Spray had introduced Dan to the chiefs of operation at the Cybersecurity and Infrastructure Agency. Dan and Jo agreed that Onetelcall's unique abilities should be available to those contacts and that a specialist division should be set up in the company to help in the invisible, intangible fight.

"Max," said Dan, "Jo and I have something we'd like to run by you. It affects the company, and it affects you." He explained his plans to weigh into the battle against cyber criminals.

For no reason at all, Jo shivered.

3

When Gary downed his early-morning Bloody Mary after passing out the night before, at his expulsion party, Chrissie first recognised an imperfection in her son. Alcohol had become a danger, a threat to the vicarious happiness she derived from his life. She blamed herself. She had been indulgent and now regretted the innumerable times she had plied her son with wine, beer and even brandy to keep him in her company when she needed the consolation his presence afforded her.

After his expulsion party black-out, Chrissie resolved to wean her boy off the bottle. It was too late. He found what she hid, he hid what she didn't find. Gary Jnr was hooked, and Chrissie had no solution. Gary's need to please his mother led him to make promises he knew he couldn't keep. Time and time again, he assured her that he'd got his drinking under control, usually when he'd had a taster or two for courage. He knew, as he spoke, that his promises were illusory. His intention to appease his mother was real, but his intention to stop drinking was not. To Gary, lying was instinctive and automatic, his use of deception was spontaneous. He had become a typical alcoholic; special, different, excluded, misanthropic, unempathetic and a deceitful liar. His decline was fast and calamitous. From needing a morning drink, he soon had to get up several times through the night for a drink to make the shakes, sweats and nightmares go away. From being able to do some studying on his laptop, he became incapable of concentrating for more than a few minutes. His hands shook, his appetite disappeared, and his bowels became a sluice.

As the addiction worsened, he stayed in bed. He couldn't walk without draping himself over his mother's shoulders and shuffling behind her resolute support. He couldn't co-ordinate. He had no balance. He listened to the sound of morning traffic and wondered how people did it. He looked at the stairs and knew he couldn't control his legs to go down them. His physical and mental dependency was so strong, so frightening, that Chrissie knew she had no choice but to give him the alcohol he so desperately needed. She knew it was killing him. She could feel in her heart, her leaden heart, that she would soon be burying her boy. No mother should have to bury her son, she cried to herself, but she knew it to be a reality.

Initially, the GP was no help. 'Tell him to stop drinking' was the first advice she got. A mother in fear of losing her baby is not easily put off. She found a GP in another practice who understood alcoholism and who would help her. After a difficult consultation with her semi-drunk son, the GP outlined a strategy that involved Librium and a complete cessation of any booze under Chrissie's supervision.

It took a great deal of Librium, often six tablets at a go, to keep Gary from having fits. After four days, it was working, and Gary showed signs of returning to the world as a human being. Chrissie was as astonished as she was thrilled.

Gary stayed off the booze for thirteen days, with the help of diminishing quantities of pills. On the fourteenth day, he felt well enough to venture outside and into town. It was a hot day, he was thirsty and, surely, a can of cold cider wasn't like real drinking, he thought as he bought one. Chrissie immediately smelled Gary's tell-tale breath. They tried again with another regime of Librium and an alcohol-free, home-based cure. Again, Gary soon responded and even began to find an appetite again. Stronger and feeling so much better, Gary Jnr volunteered to do some shopping for his mother. From the moment he stepped out of the house, he knew what he was going to do. He remembered the cider aroma trap and instead, poured a half bottle of vodka into a fizzy orange drink. And he felt good. The glow, warmth and fuzziness satiated him as his cerebral cortex became affected by the alcohol. Filled with positivity and confidence, he wanted to mollify his mother.

"I'm strong enough to beat it," came the words. Chrissie wondered why all drunks think that vodka has no smell. She wondered how words and meanings could differ so much. She recognised self-delusion in her son. She could feel his need to be placatory and felt a fleeting pleasure from it, but she knew he didn't, couldn't, deliver on his promise. The time had come for a final, precipitous action. She would save his life if it killed her. She searched the internet and found a name. 'There is an answer to alcohol addiction' read the entry, 'To talk, call this number'.

She called.

At 10.00 the next morning, a large, bearded man settled into the larger of Chrissie's sitting room sofas. Gary, grey-faced and stubbly, and still in his dressing gown was holding a glass of red wine. He was on his second bottle of the morning so far. He looked at the man with trepidation; he seemed like some sort of nemesis. The man looked at him with benign understanding, and Gary relaxed a little.

"I'm Ian, I'm an alcoholic," said the smiling beard. "I'm here to help you. All you have to do is want me to help you. If you do, I will. If you don't, then probably, you are beyond any help. Looking at you now, I'd suspect you are close to being beyond any redemption, but it's up to you. Do you want to give it a go, or have I wasted my time?"

Gary's numb mind fumbled to make sense of what he'd just heard. He hadn't expected to be confronted so directly. He wanted sympathy, understanding and a gentle word of encouragement, not a frontal attack.

Ian knew what Gary was experiencing and why. He decided to go further.

"Confused are you, Gary? Wanted me to say there, there it will be alright? Pretend it's just a little illness that will pass. Perhaps give you an easy way out. A couple of drinks a day will be fine, and you'll do that, won't you?"

Gary seized on the last few words. "Yes, I could do that," he replied to this odd, affronting, disquieting stranger. "That's the answer, isn't it, just a couple a day and I'll be back to normal in no time, eh?"

Chrissie shrugged in despair and then shot a look of stark, hopeless desperation at Ian. He smiled again and, for once, Chrissie felt comforted.

"No more dancing around the flowers, Gary, it's time. This morning it's time for some truths. And I'm the chap to deliver those truths. Why? You ask. Why am I the deliverer of such an ultimatum, like live or die? What gives me the right? I'll tell you.

"I was you. Eighteen years ago, and probably about your age, I was just as you are now. I was dying. I was killing those who love me. I was a drunk, a lush, a dipso, a pisshead. I lied, cheated, and stole. I lost my money, my home, my car, my friends and my family. I lost me. I'd lost the will to live or the strength to die, the ability to go on and the never-ending, terrible, all-consuming, overwhelming need for another drink. Recognise any of that, Gary?"

Chrissie saw a tear trace down her son's cheek as he nodded. Nemesis or saviour, wondered Gary as he said,

"If you were once me, you are me talking now, you are my feelings and my thoughts, I don't know how or why, but that's it, that's exactly it."

Chrissie cried. Ian's smile widened into a happy beam.

"Gary, do you want to tell me that you are an alcoholic and you'd rather not be? Do you want to tell your mum that you now know you are an addict, that you suffer from an illness called alcoholism and that you will let me help you? Will you trust me now, before I even tell you what will happen next? Can you accept that this is the day when you resolve, once and for all time to give up the drink, to do whatever you have to do to be rid of your burden? Are you going to get real and stop killing your mother and destroying yourself?"

"Ok, ok, I give in!" Gary almost shouted as if he was in an evangelical meeting. "I'm deep in the shit, I'm a waste of space and time. You're going to save me 'cos you're a bloody walking marvel. But Ian, Ian the alco, I don't think you can help me because, here's the thing you see, I can't stop. I know I can't stop. I've tried. I've done the Librium thing and it didn't work. So, much as I'd love you to save me from myself, I'm afraid you're too late, a long time too late. I'm delighted, I really am, that you found a way to stop drinking, but even though you say what I feel, you speak the words I want to say but can't, you are not me in one important aspect; you were able to stop, I am absolutely incapable of giving it up."

Chrissie's cries of hope turned to gasps of shuddering grief.

"Gary, I remember saying almost the same thing to the man who came to me to do what I would like to do for you. I didn't believe for one moment that I could rid myself of my addiction. Honestly, and I bet this is in your mind too, I wasn't even sure I wanted to say goodbye to my best friend, my constant companion; it would be worse than losing a loved one. But I was wrong, very wrong. I was in every bit as bad a state as you are; I was just as addicted and dependent as you are. I had no belief, no compulsion other than to have another drink – which, I can see, is what you are doing right now."

Gary filled his glass again for the third time since the man had arrived.

"Yeah? Well, hooray for you, Mr Big. I'm not big, I'm not strong, I'm not you or anyone else who has cracked it, am I?"

"No, you're not, at least not yet. But you heard my words, you heard yourself through me, and you know, deep down, you are beyond desperate to get off it. All you lack is the ability to see yourself without a drink, imagine life without drinking, and have the confidence in yourself to achieve what others have achieved and what I'm sure you could too. But, remember this, Gary, always remember this, there is no cure, no magic formula, no silver bullet here. You are an alcoholic and you'll always be an alcoholic. You can choose to be a dead alcoholic or an alcoholic who chooses not to drink. That's it, the bus you were on no longer runs."

Chrissie feared that Gary had slipped into some sort of coma. He was motionless, glass in hand, cheeks wet and shining, eyes fixed on Ian, but no words came from his mouth. There was no movement, not even the rise and fall of breathing, for what seemed like hours. Finally, his voice returned,

"Ian, when your 'Ian' came to you, like some visitation from on high, did he frighten you, did he try to break you, did he make you feel like a worthless piece of shit?"

"What happened to me, Gary is exactly what's happening to you. I have done nothing mystical; I've only spoken what you know to be right and true. You are feeling worthless because that's your own opinion of yourself. I am not trying to break you, as you seem to think, just overcome the power of your addiction and penetrate that maelstrom mind. Yes, I'd like to break the hold your addiction has over you, but I don't want to break you. I want you to take this chance of rebuilding yourself."

Gary's gaze did not leave Ian, but he fell silent again. Neither mother nor visitor could read his thoughts; Gary didn't understand what he was thinking anyway. Disconnected images, feelings, dreams and fears torrented through his fazed brain. Wherever his mind meandered, he could see a pinpoint light of life, he would later call it the original beacon of hope, and he knew he was in a futile fight with inevitability.

"Ok, Ian, you've got me this far, what's next? Tell me what happens now, how do I achieve the impossible, how do I give up what I can't give up? Tell me that, and I'm all yours."

Ian sighed the relief of a man reprieved from hanging. Chrissie's crying changed back from anguish to joy.

"Good man, Gary, good man. Let me give you what I suggest should happen. From what your mum has told me and what I've seen today, I can tell you that you are in for a long, hard grind to recovery. You've got to want it, not for your mum, not to please other people, not because you feel you should but because you want to get your life back more than anything. If that's the case, you'll make it, but it will take a lot of help along the way, starting with rehab."

Ian described a place he knew where addiction treatment was at its best and most successful. It was expensive, costing more per week than most people earn, but if anything could work, this would. Chrissie nodded through the payment without demur. Ian called the residential rehab, and after less than two hours of walking through the front door, he had arranged for his stricken client to get the help he so obviously and urgently needed.

Two days later, Gary Jnr sat in his mother's car outside the grand old mansion that was the rehab, draining what, he now believed, would be his last bottle of wine. Finally fortified, he stumbled in.

4

Over several weeks, Dan and Jo had meetings with some of the top cyber-crime agency heads, from the UK, Europe and America. They had expected post-Brexit reluctance from the European cyber security bodies but found nothing but co-operation, openness, and enthusiasm. "We leave politics and posturing to those who play such games. Meanwhile, we continue to work to allow them that freedom," said one EU technologist pithily.

They also met the best of the world's leading cyber security companies. Some of these were Onetelcall competitors, but Dan believed they would come together impartially to fight for the greater good and, perhaps, benefit commercially too. Their initial conversation fell into three categories. Prevention came first, followed by attack management and recovery. Third, came a topic few had actively embraced: tracking and locating the sources of incursions - or peeling the onion, as Dan put it in an allusion to the Tor browser, entry-level access to the dark web.

From the outset, Dan had stressed his case for complete discretion about his initiative. Those invited to the discussions were asked not to pass on any information, not even in their own companies or organisations. The Alliance agreed that it might admit a specific person with a particular skill but, as the companies and agencies involved all knew they had moles, spies and intelligence pirates, they agreed to absolute confidentiality and secrecy.

It was over a dinner that looked like a reunion of old chums having a good night out that the foundations were laid and agreed upon. This time they were in Athens, home to ENISA, the European cyber-security agency. They had selected an intimate restaurant where their reservation for twelve carried a request for the exclusive use of the compact, ancient cellar dining area. No eavesdroppers and the impenetrable stone walls and ceiling excluded listening devices.

Their virtual Alliance, unlike the well-known Five Eyes, had no name; it was wraith-like, with no tangible substance and as invisible and imperceptible as its quarry. It had no formal communication, no public face and no industry presence. It shunned the plethora of cybersecurity conferences, summits and conventions. Each member would deny its existence if asked. Unless one of the twelve was a most adept fifth columnist, they were as leakproof as they could be.

There was a consensus that the combined global effort in providing tools and services to thwart cybercrime, an activity that involved all members in varying roles, was healthy and, on occasion, inspired. However, the stark truth was that for every advance the good guys made, the baddies could do better. In the battle for good against evil, the white hats were getting toughed up by the black hats.

The new Alliance would, members agreed, set about identifying the miscreants, their locations and their paymasters. They would have to be strategic in deploying their limited resources. One team would look at the cyberattack favourites of malicious domains, malware and ransomware, whilst another would work on email and social media-based hacking and large-scale misinformation, manipulation and destructive influence. Phishing, identity theft, virus and spam, attachment malware and trojan horse planting all fell into his remit, as did social media dangers such as social engineering, fake accounts, celebrity spoofing, fake links and information leakage. Too many threats, too many perpetrators. Dan would lead this effort from his Onetelcall main offices in Olderbury and would, as agreed by the Alliance members, have Jo and Max working with him.

To accommodate this new imperative, Dan restructured the company to make himself chairman, Max CEO, Harvey Schuster, a Spray recruit of outstanding ability and evident probity, as the US and manufacturing COO with the ever-faithful Karl and Chloe in Europe, also acting as joint COOs. To thicken the smokescreen, Dan announced a new Onetelcall function, an understandable and logical reaction to the massive rise in Pandemic cybercrime, a Cyber-forensic unit he would oversee with Jo as its lead driver.

Many of the Onetelcall employees in Olderbury knew Jo; they knew what she had suffered. They knew about the relationship between Dan and Jo, but none of them saw it as marital nepotism. Jo's undoubted skills were acknowledged, and those seconded to the forensic unit were happy to work with her. Even with the resources of Onetelcall, Jo had to limit the scope of her enquiries; only significant events from the start of the pandemic would be chosen. She concentrated effort on cases where identity theft had enabled cybercrime in larger companies where a sufficiently sophisticated IT infrastructure could be forensically scrutinised.

Jo's life had been glamourous for most of her working life apart from being attacked on her own doorstep. She had worked for an IT consultancy, Raglan Inc, to create and deliver special events. She then progressed to running her own company providing unique experiences for clients with the healthiest of budgets. She had flown first or business class around the world, staying in the best hotels, meeting fascinating people, eating the best food, and tasting the best wines. She knew that heading up a forensic cybercrime unit might not be so chic and sophisticated, but she wasn't prepared for the junior detective grind her new role demanded.

It seemed like an endless trail. She visited companies where identity fraud had resulted in a major loss for both the company and the person whose identity had been stolen. She visited football clubs and traced tweets encouraging mass hooliganism or racial abuse. She was allowed by some newspapers to inspect the readers' comments files and data; she explored the IT departments of the two major universities willing to accept such investigation and analysed the provenance of some of its more political and radical posts and mails. Her hunt for cyber-thugs led her to places she'd never dreamed of visiting.

From hard, physical evidence captured from various social media platforms, Jo kept copies of the more insidious, inciting or iniquitousness. Digital evidence was gathered, copied and distributed to specialists in the Alliance where banks of code-crunching machines looked to find clues to country, hacker-farm, location and, in some cases, authors and code writers. Word-based examples were analysed by Jo's team and specialists in the Alliance who concentrated on social media-driven subversion. In what had become a powerful and technically sophisticated global industry, hackers and social media trolls often made surprisingly elementary mistakes, including amateur misuse of whatever language their targets spoke, traces from incorrect character sets and keyboards and many an idiomatic howler. Errors were, however, so far very rarely sufficient to give a clue to the perpetrator's identity.

After three months of diligent examination, the Alliance was making some progress. Comprising, as it did, several companies which excelled in cyber-security, it had been possible to get a couple of steps ahead of the hackers, for a short while anyway.

Harvey Schuster, in his new Onetelcall forensic suite, had, with the Alliance's approval, put together an elite of hackers. In a deal with the Attorney General's Department, the recruits had avoided jail by changing sides, or hats, to become white hat hackers, as the good guys were called. They had concentrated on data breaches, mainly because half of the global data breaches occurred in the US. These incursions had created havoc and disaster for targeted companies, wiping millions off stock prices and costing millions in repair. Costs escalated further when ransomware was involved with often disastrous PR results as the public lost faith in the afflicted company's ability to keep customers' account details safe.

One of Harvey's innovations, shared throughout the Alliance, was an ingenious 'Trojan Mare'.

"You know, it's like this damn Covid virus," explained Harvey to Dan, "codes, like molecules, all have hooks and innate attractions, that's how they embed themselves. Well, our trojan mare is some bitch on heat, I can tell you. Some goddam hacker geek in a god-forsaken Chinese sweat cell comes up with yet another trojan horse virus, our girl swishes her tail, shows her credentials and, wham, that horny old virus is so attracted to her, he hooks up with her and before you know it, he's fubar. And here's the kicker, it's a patch written in our best invention, a sort of code-Esperanto, so our mare bats her eyelashes at any old horse, whether its Ruby, Java, C++, Leet-geek lash-up, Python, well whatever."

It was an early success, but Dan and the Alliance knew it was at King Canute's level in the face of the tsunami of attacks.

"Harv's code-blind equine tart is a great coup," said Dan to Jo and Max in their Olderbury board room, "but even I didn't realise what we were getting into when I first thought about this Alliance. Since then, since this terrible pandemic took its grip, we've seen cyber-attacks of all types and varieties mushroom by well over six hundred per cent and, you know, it's continuing to grow at a helluva rate. Do you know, ransomware alone is now costing over twenty billion worldwide? And it's expanding at a phenomenal rate. I'm not even going to list all the threats we and the Alliance face, it is so much more than when we first talked. I'm getting to the stage where I don't know which way to go; it's all so bloody overwhelming,"

"I've got to agree, boss," said Max, "but it's great for our business. I was talking to our northern region customer services chief, you know her, Stella Edmonds came to us from IBM; well, she described her life at the moment as selling by rejection. She has so many new businesses requests that she's putting them through a vetting process before even seeing them."

"Just as well," replied Dan, "'cos my big idea about hacker and troll-hunting is eating money and resources like a hungry Labrador, and I know the same is true for our commercial Alliance colleagues. Of course, our state and government-run agency colleagues don't have to worry as much, so they are now picking up a lot of the expensive strain."

"I know," said Max, "I've been juggling resources here, and in the US and Europe to keep up with customer demand and meet the Alliance's needs too. Right now, my suggestion would be that each Alliance member specialises in a particular threat and discipline and, for a change, Jo and I have an idea to run past you, Dan, before you lay another one of yours on us."

"What's this? Independent thinking, I'm not sure I allow that! Been plotting behind my back, Jo?" said Dan, smiling happily.

"Behind your back Danny boy? What could you be imagining?" replied Jo with an affected coquettish air. "Max and I have nothing to declare, except our genius, of course, and just because we've been putting our heads together doesn't mean you've got anything to worry about… yet."

Max blushed slightly; Dan snorted his harrumph.

"Thanks, Jo," Max recovered his composure, "but we have been doing some thinking, boss, and given all Jo's work so far and the progress we have been making, we think the Onetelcall Alliance forensic unit should concentrate on email and social media threats. There are two reasons for this. One is that we believe these two open-door routes to both cybercrime and social, um, engineering if that's what it's called. Second, because Onetelcall is relatively new into this market at a corporate level, so it makes commercial sense to become the de facto experts as soon as we can."

Jo was keen to pick up the story.

"I haven't mentioned this before, at home or anywhere, but I want it to be a joint effort with Max and I running it on behalf of the Alliance and, of course, Onetelcall. That means that Max will spend less time on our business and more on Alliance work. Can we cover that, Dan?"

"What, while we are running at an unprecedented level of customer demand? I don't know. My first duty is, of course, to the success of Onetelcall, but as the Alliance was my original idea, I have a duty to that too. I have to say what I don't want to say, but I think I might have to take a step back from the Alliance grunt work and pick up the reins here; that way Max will have the time he needs to get up to all sorts with my wife."

"Please don't boss, you know I've got a very low guilt threshold after all that Duggie and druggie rigmarole."

Max was referring to Duggie Miller, the delivery and collection intermediary Sniff Taylor used to pick up drugs sent into the UK via Onetelcall's goods delivery system. Duggie, also innocent in the scheme of villainy, was later given a job in logistics.

"But freeing me up makes more sense than might first appear," continued Max. "All the Alliance cyber-crime specialists are busy working on the big-ticket items, you know, like risk management, architecture, authentication processes, vulnerabilities, data security, incident management techniques and so on. But since the dramatic rise in work-from-home, hot desking, remote collaboration and virtual teams, the hackers' dreams have come true because they can access personal and corporate data, laptops, PC and networks all via simple email."

"It's staggering Dan," added Jo, "what we've found over the last weeks has been eye-opening, no wonder hackers have such an easy time. People working from home don't apply the same security precautions as they would in an office. They leave their machines running with open ports to, say, the internet, printers, social media feeds, RSS feeds, and other routes too. They use the same passwords for multiple accounts – and these are often golden oldie favourites like 'password123' or 654321!, QWERTY, 111111 and 000000 like common factory defaults."

"Most people don't take email seriously," said Max, continuing the double act. "It is by far the most common form of communication globally, after talking and texting. Whether it's on services like Gmail or Outlook or corporate secure email servers, most folk just don't take even mundane steps to protect themselves. Sometimes news headlines have a salutary effect, like tales of sextortion, but most people turn a blind eye to reports of phishing, malware seeding, spam, identity theft, common extortion, ransom, malicious intent, spyware and on and on and on, just so many threats and so little awareness."

"It's the same with malicious social media trolling and fakery," said Jo. "Character assassination, bullying and vile, anonymous trolling are just the starters. You'd never believe what I found out at the universities, for instance. It's called social engineering but actually, it is brainwashing with menaces. Race, gender, politics, religion, they've all become topics of extreme manipulation where opinion is heavily influenced and disagreement is bullied, or cancelled, or driven to suicide, until everyone toes the line regardless of their inner thoughts."

"I know, I know," said Dan, "but we are Onetelcall, we are part of the Alliance, and our job is to provide technical solutions and systemic processes that cause the malevolent minorities to lose their power. We are not, repeat not, crime busters. Max and I know first-hand what social media manipulation can achieve. We know how easy it is to steal identity, post fake posts, create fake videos and hijack the whole social media world to create mayhem. That's what I want to fight. I don't think we can do anything else, and we certainly can't become self-appointed guardians of virtual crime."

"You say that young fella-me-lad," answered Jo, "but I'm not so sure we can't do more. I believe we can get further than anyone has so far in tracing, tracking, and even identifying some of the most malicious, evil and harmful emails and social media trolling and hacking facilities. Not all of them, not even many of them but some, maybe just one, two, three or so, but it's a start and it has to be done."

"Dan, the thing is, your wife and I have been turning detective a bit and we think we are onto something. We think we might be able to dig into an eastern European hacker factory that attacks newspaper comment sections, all email, populist topics on Twitter, Tik-Tok, WhatsApp, YouTube, WeChat and, lately, more on MeWe too. They also intrude on most popular interactive game sites, so the girl in Tokyo who plays Battle and

Legend games with you in a multi-player league is, in reality, a hairy-arsed commie exile with an axe to grind. And we think we know how to find him and his hundreds of colleagues who bang out malice, disruption and malevolence by the ton every day and night."

"Look, Dan," Jo sounded imploring, "we agree that it will be technology and global cooperation that will eventually curtail this loathsome activity, but in the meantime, the fight is too one-sided for my liking. When minorities get the upper hand and no one fights back, disaster and conflict are bound to follow. History shows us that. Now is the time for the majority to be championed, and if Max and I can start another ball of backlash rolling, then I, for one, believe we should, we must."

Max picked up the argument, "We aren't saying we can call out the state-sponsored organisations in China, Iran and all the other known places, but we can have a go at the low-life criminals, the cyber-thugs and extortionists, the pirates and mercenary black-hat keyboard soldiers who proliferate in the Eastern European countries. We think we've spotted one and can expose it. It is a massive anti-everything money-making racket in Moldova."

5

Behind the heavy, wide oak doors of Harbour House, a rehabilitation and treatment centre on the south coast, Gary was welcomed by a slight young woman who looked an unlikely gatekeeper in such a facility.

"Guzzled your last drink, I see then Gary?" smiled Kate, the receptionist, as Gary steadied himself against the countertop. "Well, that's ok. Normally we don't accept admittances who've been drinking but, from what Ian has told us, I'm not surprised to see you like this. We'll process you now but probably it's best if you stay in the medic wing tonight and your work with us can begin tomorrow when are more, er more shall we say compos mentis?"

Harbour House was a magnificent eighteenth-century mansion built with traditional Georgian symmetry for a wealthy shipowner. The house and grounds, abandoned on the ship owner's death, had been a monastery, a first world-war hospital, a second world war US command post and a girls' boarding school until it was refurbished as a residential treatment home in the early 1970s. Offering treatment for a range of addictions, drug, alcohol, gambling, sex, and various food and eating disorders, Harbour House, HH as it was called, worked on the Minnesota Model of abstinence treatment based on the Alcoholics Anonymous 12-Step programme. Over 7,000 addicts had been treated at HH by the time Gary arrived. The facility boasted the highest success rate in Europe, although there was always much discussion as to what qualified as a success.

Gary would have had a choice of a short-term detoxification stay or a minimum of a twelve-week stay with further secondary and third-stage programmes available after his initial three-month treatment. He didn't have a choice as Ian and Chrissie had made it clear he would be there for the full twelve weeks at a very minimum. He would join the house's other forty or so men and women of various backgrounds and ages, who shared his problem, his illness, his addiction to whatever was killing them slowly. Booze and betting, drugs and sex were no respecters of social standing, seniority or intelligence or achievement. HH had welcomed lords and ladies, stars and celebrities, QCs and judges, MPs and journalists, actors and film-makers, in fact, the gamut of human life and types.

Totally egalitarian, HH also provided hope and treatment for what the inmates referred to as 'jail-swervers', those who would go to jail if they did not undergo state-funded treatment. It also received regular income from unions and large-scale employers such as Transport for London and the NHS for their addict employees. Large corporates that wanted to save their ailing, burnt-out executives who had turned to drink and substances to ease the pain of their pressurised lives also provided revenue for HH. Residents, or inmates as they called themselves, shared dormitories, shared a refectory and shared the working life of the house by doing chores. These 'therapeutic duties' included food preparation, washing up, room preparation, lounge and garden tidying and other day-to-day tasks. Age and gender meant little, everyone shared burdens equally. A team of dedicated and conscientious counsellors provided psychology and compassion-based therapy; nurses and a doctor provided medical treatment and drug management. Reiki, acupuncture, mindfulness, tai-chi, qigong, and hypnotherapy added to HH's range of restorative recovery techniques.

Occasionally, patients would fit, have drug-withdrawal attacks and suffer from a range of addiction-related illnesses such as pancreatitis; for these, there was a hospital unit of six beds. It was in one of those beds that Gary awoke after his first Librium-induced sleep. He was shaking, his vision was blurred and his sense of balance totally shot. One of the nurses helped him wash and dress and put him in a wheelchair; walking was out of the question.

"Gary," said the nurse, "this is Henry, he'll be your buddy

and show you the ropes until you settle in."

Gary looked up from the wheelchair and saw a smiling face, dark brown in hue and showing scars on both cheeks. Gary felt a tremor of fear, whether it was a nervous response to lack of alcohol or the reaction to be expected from a sheltered suburban existence, he didn't know but as he looked into the large kind eyes and broad smiling features of his new friend, his initially tremulous grin gave way to a suddenly confident, friendly and hopeful chuckle.

Henry wheeled Gary to the sunny, expansive refectory. It was set out, self-service style, in four rows of twelve with a smaller separate table which, as Gary would learn, was for the elder of the house. This senior role was held by the person who'd been there longest, week by week; the leader had four therapy house group leaders as tablemates.

"Coffee, Gary?"

"Henry, I'd remember you in my will for a coffee right now. Thirsty doesn't cover it."

"Don't get excited, man. This is cash-and-carry bulk instant; it is the colour of shit and tastes that way too."

"So, you're my buddy then; how's that work?"

"Every newcomer, usually well fucked-up like you, gets given a buddy, an experienced resident to guide them around, teach them the HH ways and rules and generally help them feel as at home as being in this god-awful place ever can be."

"It's not a good place to be?"

"What's good about having to be in a rehab 'cos you've got yourself addicted to some shit or other? As far as rehabs go, this is a good one and, if you want it, you'll begin to get better here. Got to say it isn't a palace of fun though; that it certainly isn't."

Gary nodded in understanding. As he sipped his instant coffee, he reflected on this cataclysmic change in his life. There was an inevitability about it; deep down, he'd known for a long time that he'd had too passionate a love for his bottled buttress, and, in rehab, he had a chance to reclaim his life. What, he wondered, would be the opportunities for a man with his talents in this peculiar environment? Would it be like school; find the strongest and make them allies, spot the weakest and exploit them?

"At the risk of being a bit non-PC," said Gary lightly to his new buddy, "you don't look like a Henry?"

"S'ok man, I'm not one of your touchy precious immigrants and my name isn't really Henry; I've just always been called that as a sort of nickname."

"How come?"

"It's after a missionary called Henry Townsend. He was one of your presbyterian ministers who thought he'd spread the word of God to us natives." Henry paused for a short, ironic chuckle and continued, "He ended up, after travelling from Sierra Leone through Guinea, Cote d'Ivoire, Ghana, Togo and Benin at my home of Ogun state in Nigeria. He worked at the Yoruba mission where he and a fella called Freeman were the first Europeans to set foot in our region, so they were pretty famous."

Gary nodded again, with partly feigned and partly genuine interest.

"So, old Henry did his missionary work in Abeokuta, our main town, and he was a popular chap; he wrote hymns and he and his wife did a lot of teaching. Anyway, the thing about the nickname is that Henry Townsend started a newspaper. I think it was the start of Nigeria's print industry, or whatever. Henry's paper was the first bilingual newspaper in the country and, you see, when I was young, I wanted to be a reporter, a Woodward or Bernstein, so my family called me Henry after him which is, it must be said, easier than my real name which is Akintoye."

"I see, yep, Henry does trip off the tongue a bit more readily," said Gary hoping he sounded enthusiastic. He needed to be in his buddy's good books in these early days. "Did you make it? Did you become a reporter?"

Henry looked agitated.

"I shoulda," he said with a trace of bitterness. "I had all the breaks. My father was an ambassador, and I went to an international school in Paris where I was taught well and had a lot of introductions to the Paris news and media world. Trouble was, and you'll know this, most of those people, men and women both, all drink like they're about to be abandoned in the middle of the Sahara and I didn't need to be asked twice to join in."

"Never made it then eh?"

"Tell you what, man, I'm a walking waste of space. I had opportunities and lost them, threw them away. I was a proud man, Gary, and I have these to prove my heritage." Henry ran his hand over his six scars, three on each cheek, "Now I've been disowned, my parents don't want to know me, my old friends ignore me, and the women I've known don't know me anymore. I never got a job; I got a criminal record instead. I fucked up, Gary, that's the story, the only story, I just fucked up because of the booze."

He was one hundred and ninety centimetres tall and weighed 96 kilograms; he was strong and intimidating, but Akintoye's shoulders shuddered, his head bent, and, against Gary's wheelchair-bound shoulders, he cried tears of utter desolation.

Gary and Henry became better than appointed buddies; they found an affinity although, to Gary's surprise and disappointment, Henry was a man of some integrity and honour who had a desperate need to find ways of earning others' respect again. Some of the other HH inmates had no such need for approbation, priding themselves on their respective levels of immorality and dishonesty. There was a hierarchy amongst the jail-swervers and addiction-driven recidivists, with status being established according to who could tell the best tales of the worst egregious adventures. Gary took his time to select those with whom he could plan and plot and those who were rehab's equivalents of swots and teacher's pets. He doubted that there was much profit to be made in the confines of the house but, with his mind on life after rehab, he contrived a preliminary recruitment programme for likely lieutenants.

He favoured The Prof. Every rehab has a 'prof', usually highly qualified chemists from university or large pharmaceutical companies who had augmented their income by creating and producing designer drugs. Too often, they became victims of their own creation. HH's Prof probably had a name but nobody seemed to know it; even the staff called him Prof. Late forties, looking like late seventies, he had avoided a prison sentence by accepting rehab. Prof's constant companion in HH was a man known as Bob, after Bob Martin's dog worming pills, because of his propensity to take any tablet he could find, including those he used to buy for his pets. Bob was younger and better looking than Prof, but he had suffered from the pills and his mental agility was diminished.

Slightly slower wit didn't deter Daria from chasing Bob; she was Moldovan and found Bob's slow speech a relief and respite from the rapid-fire Gatling gun conversations much favoured by addicts. Daria was in her mid-thirties, assisted blond, lithe and supple with a graceful, elegant, slight physique that men found irresistible in either a protective or just plain lustful way. Bob wasn't sure whether he was 'smitten or smutten', but he loved having her as frequent company. HH house rules frowned on fraternisation and had strictly enforced boundaries between the male and female residents. Bob had no intention of breaking the rules but enjoyed the gossip suggesting that he transgressed several boundaries most nights.

When Daria first spotted Gary, he had risen from his wheelchair, graduated from buddydom and was benefitting, physically at least, from the HH 'work, eat, sleep regime'. Striding alongside his chum Henry, Gary looked fitter and more alert than he had for some years. Daria saw something in Gary that others did not; she saw something akin to her own inner venality and licentiousness.

During the warm sunny weeks of incarceration, Gary and

Daria lived in their fantasy, as characters in an HH story. Some of the story was reality and some just childlike make-believe. In his early stages of recovery, escapism was perfect for Gary, who was beginning to regard the future, life after HH, with increasing trepidation. The realities written into this shared novella were, thought Gary, almost as unreal as the fantasy. Daria, he learned, was a mole.

"Really? What? You fuckin kidding me? You joking or what?"

Daria put her finger to her lips to quieten Gary's astonished exclamations on hearing that she had been planted in HH deliberately.

6

The Covid pandemic had created global turmoil. In the east, suppression and displays of territorially aggressive state power featured almost daily in the western press. In the west, discord and disharmony spread faster than the virus itself. Conspiracy theories ruled the social platforms. Misinformation, fake news and mendacious posts equivalent to the entire works of Shakespeare spewed out from the corrupting miscommunication ecosystem. Created in factories of fakery, destabilising and downright dangerous content fell into seven main categories – false content, false connection, manipulated content, fabricated content, misleading content, imposter content and, with increasing effect, satire and parody. Exponential penetration was achieved by motivating the younger and more impressionable and mobilising easily identified factions, pressure groups and egocentric drum-bangers. Aided by the multiplication of messages via troll and bot factories, falsehoods became accepted truths simply by the power of constant presence and repetition.

There is nothing more vicious than the spurned idealist and, as each socially outraged movement was shown to have spurious or gainful foundations, far away from the high principles it propounded, many supporters, hurt by being so duped and cynically manipulated, turned against their false idols. They took to alternative platforms to express their disillusionment, but it was not enough. Even combined with the silent majority, it would never be enough. Alternative platforms didn't have the firepower, and the silent majorities were silent because collectively, they didn't have the skills or resources to mount counter-misinformation campaigns. The false was becoming the truth and the truth was becoming less and less accepted and acceptable in the social media-swamped world.

Dan sometimes considered the futility of his struggle. Whatever Max and Jo found, no matter how innovative and technically advanced the Alliance might be, nothing would stem the flow of malicious communication and insidious brainwashing of the millions upon millions of willing victims. With only a little help and some information gleaned from the darker side of the web, he and Max had been able to shanghai and commandeer the platforms for their own purposes of visiting their form of justice on an evil, malicious and repugnant thug. How could his meagre efforts now prevent others far more powerful and sophisticated from doing their worst?

Dan had written a paper for the Alliance's consideration. It was nothing new, a reiteration of the need to step up global cooperation in the battle against the bots, trolls, farms, factories, and networks of spreaders of mass deception. He claimed it was up to the Alliance members, agencies, cybercrime companies, platforms and manufacturers to rise up as one and execute a clear strategy, from education on spotting fake emails and posts and limiting the reposting of damaging material, to the production of bio-sensitive technology, which could be employed to check users' eyes or an advanced polygraph style device for authentication before posts could be published on the social media platforms. He knew he was wading out of his depth in some of the areas of technology development and that new security and veracity developments that were far beyond even his understanding were in beta testing at the time of his Alliance paper.

One principle Dan supported had little to do with technology and innovation; It was about anonymity, traceability and accountability. Jo's view of the whole fallacious email and posting threat was that you kill the snake by biting its head off. Every emailer and social media user who re-posts, repeats or passes on spurious content was aiding and abetting the originator, knowingly or not. She maintained education and awareness were crucial but finding and exposing the farms and factories and identifying the miscreant lone wolves and hunting packs had to be the focus. She could see the arguments for anonymity, which led to some rorty boardroom discussions.

"I know it's a well-aired argument," she said during one of their frequent board table conversations on the matter, "but many a whistle-blower has been grateful for social media anonymity and a lot of good, a lot of justice, a lot of identifying wrong-doers, oppressors, deviants and perverts, a lot of people on the take and a great deal of misuse of power has been exposed because of it."

"I agree," nodded Dan as, annoyingly for Jo, he often did when their views differed, "and it's a disgrace that in the twenty-first century, people are still forced into anonymous tale-telling to get a wrong righted. There should be avenues anyone can pursue to make a complaint and expose corruption or bullying or whatever without having to resort to social media in its increasing dodginess. There is so much rubbish out here now that soon none of the platforms will be credible for any whistleblowing, anonymous or not."

"It's a global problem though, isn't it?" suggested Jo, "I mean, what about people in authoritarian countries where regimes track social media and where, if you say something that isn't approved of, you get a visit from the stormtroopers and made to disappear or get banged up? For some of those people being able to post anonymously is the only way they can communicate with the outside world. In places like that where censorship and surveillance rule, free speech has been kyboshed; human rights, human problems and human atrocities are hidden from the world by social media subjugation. If there is an argument for keeping anonymity, surely, it is this?"

"Yeah, you've got a good point," agreed Dan again. "I know that anonymity on the net has been a lifeline for people suffering from all kinds of barbarism and persecution, despotism and even genocide. The thing is, Jo, the world knows about most of these abominations and iniquities, so social media isn't the only crucial, pivotal tool in the fight to bring awareness to the world. Where anonymity is singularly culpable is bringing hate, bias, prejudice and cruelty into a communication medium that was originally developed to enable friendship and closeness. The irony is, I think, that so much vile, base and vicious content comes from the very states that ban free speech. Look at it, Jo, Max, the sheer weight of posts that undermine national policies, governments, companies and culture, that attack and pervert human rights, inclusion and diversity, so much ganged-up cyberbullying, it all comes from places where life is cheap, and freedoms are denied. Because of the constant flood of misinformation, so many groups of people in the West are now in thrall to the manipulative, subversive messaging dictated and trolled out from Russia, China, Iran, and all the usual suspects. We'll never eradicate it, of course, but traceability, accountability and real identity would be a good start."

"My big worry," said Jo, "and it is so evident from what Max and I have been seeing recently, is how organised and orchestrated so much email and social media incursion is. You know, and I believe it, over half of all messages on all the platforms sent to footballers in the UK were racist, gender-driven or just straight depraved and, they reckon, cracking on for ninety per cent of those were anonymous and, what we've seen in our tracking, is that they come from outside the UK even if they are tagged something like 'footyfan from Farnborough', truth is it's more likely to be Dimitri the Diabolical from Minsk."

"Dimitri the Diabolical? *Really*? Oh, Jo, if it wasn't so serious it would be funny. We could have a Onetelcall competition for the best troll handles. You know, not so much Vlad the Impaler as Vanya the Vicious from Vladivostok?"

"I've always fancied being Serge the Urge…"

"Thanks, Max for your always positive contribution, you smutty so and so," smiled Jo, "but I'd have thought Max the Unready or Larry the Limp from Littlehampton might be more appropriate."

"The trouble is," said Dan, tapping the board table to bring the meeting back to order, "what you've discovered is just the tip of the iceberg. I can tell you that some of the Alliance members are reporting that it is the same troll factories, especially in eastern Europe, which combine whipping up dissent and hatred with concealed in-plain-view keyword sequences in their emails. These sequences fire up sleepers to give the hackers easy access to corporate data, usually for financial gain, they say, and it's more than simple ransomware and more than wilful disruption, it is about massive-scale fraud, records theft and identity replication."

"That's what we think too," joined in Max, "and, from what we've seen, these cyber gangs are easier to spot than the more elaborate politically sponsored and radical operators."

"How so?" asked Dan.

"Well, Dan, it's more art than science," responded Jo, picking up on Max's theme. "It looks to us as though there is a big difference in skill and intellect between the online pirate hoodlums and the seditious propaganda machines. Max and I will, won't we?" Jo glanced at Max who was nodding his agreement, "admit the awful social media campaigns that are so damaging to society are less likely to come from the smaller, eastern European operators. They are in it for the money and don't give a toss about subversion or revolution, but their emails are often pretty transparent and naive. You know the sort of thing, 'You've won a prize' or 'We tried to deliver' or any of the tried and tested ruses which encourage people to open a link."

"What's even better," added Max, "is that they all rip off logos and create imitation web pages; they even have bogus call centres to entice the unwary into revealing their information."

"Yes, that makes sense," replied Dan, "and I agree that we and the Alliance have to work at many levels because there are so many different threats. That's why big cyber agencies like our own National Cyber Security Centre are successful in being able to launch initiatives like their early-warning system, which makes corporates aware of undetected compromised networks before any damage can be done."

"That's all very well and good for high-level corporate and government departments protection," said Jo, "but what we are picking up on is the lower level, big-money scamming and cybercrime live online, and it's there where we can be more effective."

"True enough, Jo, the trouble is that the sort of cybercrime and rampant marauding you are talking about isn't really in the agencies' remits, and big companies only take notice when a malignant email to an employee, results in a major data breach. It's ok for the VPNs and security software package services, they do a good job, but they all always seem to be a step or two behind even your eastern European bandits."

"That's why Max and I think we should do more to spotlight a few of the easy-target miscreants in the hope that we kick-start a joined-up international fight against this dangerous and damaging e-crime."

Max added, "We know it's not central to the Alliance's core objectives as you originally set them out boss, nor is it particularly germane to our own business here at Onetelcall, but surely we can't waste the chance to do something against these bastards when the opportunity beckons and I, for one, well for three actually, so want to get these shits and show them what's what."

"Oh, Christ," Dan shook his head, "didn't Jo nearly getting killed on her own doorstep teach either of you anything about mixing it with the bad arses?"

"This is completely different Dan. I love you for being so protective, but it's not as though I'm going to prowl along the dark side streets of some Romanian outpost, is it? I mean, Max and I aren't turning into James Bond and Wonder Woman; we and the team are simply going to expose a troll farm by identifying them and everything that we can find that they've done. After that, it will be up to other authorities to do whatever they feel they can or should. So, it's ok, no danger, just some behind-the-scenes revelations."

"And how, my favourite Marple, do you plan on doing this? How are you, Max and the forensic team going to shine a spotlight on your Trotsky trollers? They won't take kindly to having their highly lucrative scams and schemes taken away from them by the likes of you and Max, will they? I expect they've got their own thugs and muscle and some pretty violent ways of protecting themselves; they are no different from other criminals and eastern racketeers, drug pushers and extortion mobsters, and they'll kill their brothers for a few quid, you know."

"Probably they'll have some form of protection, Dan, we know that," commented Max, "but I suspect that these skunky trollers are cowards. They probably sit in their dingy rooms, squeezing their spots and tossing themselves off every time one of their loathsome emails gets clicked. Anyway, it won't be us doing the nicking; it will, I hope, be the FBI or someone like that. Who'd be the right police force to shut down a Moldovan cybercrime farm, I wonder?"

"I suppose we'd start with going to the Alliance with the information you dig out, "replied Dan, "and see what they collectively think. And what's with this 'Moldovan', you've already started, haven't you, you've got a target in mind eh, come on Jo, Max, give me the full picture."

Jo laughed and looked slightly guilty and a little embarrassed.

"Max told me you'd spot our scheme in seconds and I should have known you would too. After all, I am your wife, and I should know you better than anyone. Perhaps I do," she grinned mischievously.

"Ok, ok, you're both very clever, so what's the story?"

"I'll tell you this, Dan," she said, "we do think that, with a bit more work and a lot of digital wizardry, we can identify a really big player in Moldova. We've separated a hefty bundle of attacks, all aimed at mega-company employees and our own civil service staff, all with the same key give-away and tell-tale indicators and all seemingly coming originally from the same source location, even if the messages do go around the world several times before reaching the dispatching servers."

"I see, Moldova, eh? And how do you think you can track…"

Max jumped back in, "and not only that, they have sometimes launched a mobile phone attack wave which one of the guys in the team - it's Samantha actually from our mobile security department, you know, marvellous eyes - I think you employed her?"

"Oh yeah, I know her, I remember interviewing her; she's the real deal on mobile stuff."

"Quite so Dan, quite so, she's amazing. I don't understand most of what she says, but, whatever, she reckons she can get a position on the original sender if the carrier co-operates which she thinks they might with a bit of crafty subterfuge. Apparently, she's done it before with them but won't tell us where, when or why. I think the carrier is either Moldcell, which is part of the Choudhary empire, or it's Orange; either way, she's confident of extracting the info. I'm not asking her anymore; she says I don't want to know, by which I think whatever her subterfuge is, it probably isn't too honest."

"So far, so good then. What put you onto this particular group of shits in the first place?"

Jo replied, "We've got fourteen organisations to study from our original Alliance agreement, six public bodies, two unis and six corporates. OK?"

"I'm keeping up," chuckled Dan.

"Good-o, and what do you think they've all got in common, especially from the pandemic?"

"Amaze me, Marple."

"They all have a large number of work-from-home and remote employees, and that's the key. This mob in Moldova have got all the email, Facebook, Twitter and especially LinkedIn tricks to fool even the savvy into some action or other that releases personal, private or sensitive information. Some are so obvious you can't believe anyone would fall for them, especially with dodgy USPs as follow-ups. Nonetheless, they do, and the gang has been massively successful in stealing huge amounts of money, in selling stolen data and records and some high-value ransom and extortion too, all from the same easy-peasy emails and simple common platform posts."

"Like what?" asked Dan.

"You'll laugh when I tell you. Hang on a mo." Jo delved into her bag and found the list she wanted. "Here you go then lover-boy, it's top of the phishing pops, and at number ten is a company Covid policy notification asking for test and trace information. At number eight, a confirmation that the recipient has been added to Microsoft Teams and should log in. Number seven is the deactivation of email in process, at six is important address code changes, number five comes in with remote work policy update, and four is scheduled server maintenance, no internet access. So on to the top three; we have Holiday Policy update, number two is a touch base on next week's meeting invitation and number one, as it would be, is the old favourite of Password Check required immediately. Neat, simple, plausible and effective, eh?"

"Then they use the obvious response prompters that most of us would act on," added Max, "there is a PayPal response required, an imitation Google unusual activity sign-in, an Adobe password refresher, a Microsoft Office document protection notice where each step in the open-it guide loads a malicious macro, a YouTube extension installer, a Facebook message and several LinkedIn attacks, including 'you've been searched – see who's looking' prompt and an AI-driven group or interest membership invitation, and so on and so on."

"You know, you two, I've been critical of general employees' gullibility but, with my guard down, I think even I'd fall for some of those scams if they were properly dressed up and house-styled. What's the giveaway tell-tale then?"

"Dan, I hate to admit it," she grinned, "but they don't take much spotting if you know what you are looking for. The follow-up web pages are often riddled with typos and mistakes. Some are written in what is obviously a translation from Russian or

Romanian, and they all have feeble USPs, often nothing like the organisation's page they are trying to be. Things like 'www.myidentcard.britain/gov.info', you know what I mean. Some show Cyrillic characters, and many use eastern European syntax and sentence structure. They don't actually sign off with dosvidaniya, but they just as well might do."

"You've got me, Jo, there's no defence, nothing I can say to stop you is there, because you're already up and running. The chase is on, I'd say. You and Max and your team are onto something worthwhile; it'll be a big prize. I just hope that the danger level is as low as you claim. Somehow, I doubt it."

7

"Why on earth, in the creation of shit, would anyone want to be a mole here for fuck's sake? What great secrets are you going to unearth, eh? Where's the value, Daria? So, you get to identify a few people who are addicts or petty criminals, hardly the stuff of spies and dead-letter drops, now is it?" Gary was sceptical.

"You don't believe, is that it, Gary? You think Daria, she lies, she makes it up?"

"Crossed my mind."

"Well, I'll tell you if you want me to tell you. You might not like what I tell. You might want to tell police what I tell. If you think you do that, I won't tell. I'll keep it only to me. If you want to know, I will tell, but you must swear to secret it. If I tell and you tell, it will be bad for you, you understand, in Moldova, we have a way with people who, what you say, squeal."

Gary was a sucker for a seductive accent; he couldn't stop looking at Daria and touching her whenever he could. His still fuddled mind was lost to her. Of course, he'd have to know, of course, he'd never tell a living soul.

"I have big family in Moldova. We work very hard. It is not easy to make living in Moldova, very poor country. We grow food, we make wine. Not much, really. My family, we grow food and make wine. Then we have club in Chisinau, our capital, and we sell food and wine. We open more clubs and sell more food and wine and we make some money. Then we make more money, and government officials want to take our money. Not tax like here, you understand. Just take money for selves. Then government official they have one of my cousins killed because he don't give them his money. They shoot him in street like rat. Everyone sees; nobody speaks; that's how it is."

"That's terrible. Didn't you go to the police?"

Daria smiled ironically.

"No. Not police. As bad as government officials. They work together. So, no. We have nobody to protect us. Just pay or get shot. That's how it is. So, we pay and we have less money. We need more and government official says he will help. Doesn't make sense, you think? They take money then help us make more money. Then they take more money. That's…"

"I know… that's how it is in Moldova. So, what happened? Did your family survive? I mean, do they still go on in the same way?"

"Yes, family survive. Government officials survive. Police survive. Family make more money but not by selling food and wine. Now we sell other things in our clubs in Chisinau. We sell cocaine, heroin, uppers, downers, designer drugs, cocktail of drugs. We make lots of money, and everyone survives very good indeed."

Gary understood all too well. He knew protection and he knew extortion.

"You not approve. You think Daria and family evil?"

"Not at all, I mean, we all have to survive, and we all do whatever we have to do to keep going and make a living. I understand completely, and I don't disapprove at all. Actually, I rather admire you and your family."

"I thought that would be so. I can tell. I thought, Gary, he knows how things are."

Gary smiled a self-effacing smile.

"So, Daria comes to HH because family want her to. I am not addict. I don't take drugs and I drink our wine only a little. Next, Daria will be Maria and go to another rehab in another town a way away from here because, by the time I go, family will not need me here anymore."

"Now you've lost me. You are saying that you go from rehab to rehab, towns that are distant from one another – but why?"

"I tell you why and this is secret. You tell, you die. I like you much but that's how it is. Would be the same if I tell police, I die. Understood?"

Gary nodded; even in his alcohol-numbed body, he felt a shudder of disquiet.

"It is this. Where there is rehab, there is addict. Where there is addict, there is pusher. Where there is pusher there is a need for drugs to be pushed. Pusher has supplier. Family takes over from supplier and we sell more drugs and make more money. That's how it…"

"Yes, yes, I get the that's how it is but- but how do you simply take over? I mean, how can your family make sure that the pushers buy from you and not from their existing suppliers? I mean, drugs, well it's a nasty business and we read about territory wars and gang fights and murders all the time. It's what causes most of the stabbings and shootings in London. You can't just waltz in and take over, can you?"

Daria looked serious.

"You say what is true. The gangs in London, they are brutal, especially the ghetto gangs. We don't fight on their playground. We find other way. We find small-time pushers, small-time dealers. Lots of them make good business, but you need lots. Best way is find them like addicts find them. In any town, pushers will know where addicts are, of course. They will push where they can sell easily. Small scale but regular and easily copied all over country. No big gangs. No turf wars. Just small scale. If a supplier gets angry and wants to stop us, family have ways of stopping them. We always win and still not big enough, deal by deal, to attract the big gangs."

Gary was impressed, "So, where do your pushers sell then?" Gary knew the answer as soon as he'd asked the question. Clever, he thought.

"Every week, sometimes two and three times, rehab addicts are taken to meetings in town. Might be AA, might be NA, might be CA. Whatever, they are all addicts in one place at one time. The addicts might be getting better, might be rehab-ing but still have need, still have want, have craving. Easy to tempt, easy to sell to, Pushers hang around at meeting places. They know the rehab addicts; they come by bus or taxi and stand together looking lost. Pushers are friends, they talk and smile and then help more by giving addicts what they want most. We make money, the officials and police make money, not just Moldova but here too."

"That's amazing," said Gary, filled with respect for such a simple, genius business method. It was right up his street, and he said so. Daria was amused, but not surprised, at Gary's enthusiasm as he asked more questions.

"But how do you get the stuff here? I mean, where does it all come from, how do you import and distribute, how do you communicate between you and the pushers? It's so clever. How does it work?"

"You don't need to know it all. I don't know to tell you all. Drugs come in from home with food and wine. Family sell lots of food and wine to UK, restaurants and hotels, they like it. Unusual and cheap, they make lots of money from us. So, drugs come in, and family friends deliver to towns with food and wine. We like towns with rehab and restaurant or hotel customers too. Good logistics. All family on Facebook and places like that. We talk to all people in the business on computer in open sight. Family very good at computer, we have business in computer in Chisinau too; government official, they like us to do computer and help up us much."

Gary gazed at Daria, her blonde hair tied back in a tight ponytail, her captivating blue eyes shone with innocence and openness, and yet here was a young girl calmly describing an enterprise of cold cunning and cynical exploitation as though she was describing her grandmother's wool shop. Was it, he wondered, Daria's intention to recruit him? Was she both mole and honey-trap? Her shrink-fit jeans reaching down to decidedly un-rehab heels, her tight shirt seductively opened to button three for a cleavage peek-a-boo all suggested a look designed to ensnare.

In some ways, Gary didn't go for self-delusion. He may believe in his invincibility and mental agility; he trusted his instinct in spotting a profit and manoeuvring people to his own ends; he knew how to enlist enforcers to bend others to his views, but was he the type of man who would make a girl like Daria go moist with libidinous wantonness? He doubted it. Gary was aware he was more tall, dark and lived-in than handsome and he reckoned, if Daria were after him, it would be for something other than his rugged looks and witty conversation. He was, he decided, about to be used, and he didn't care.

The HH common room had been the mansion's original morning room where visitors were received, and conversations held. Spacious, with views through the fine old, mullioned windows stretching over the property's lawns and well-tended flowerbeds, the room had been adapted for its new function of being a resting and chatting area for recovering addicts. In the recess to one side of the huge, Adam-style fireplace was a stack of boxed shelves, one for each resident to keep their workbooks. On the other side, the recess was occupied by a whiteboard league table that listed every inmate in order of seniority and achievement. A secondary league table kept scores of various in-house competitions between 'The Alkies', 'The Junkies' and 'The Weirdos'. The latter being a catch-all for sex, gambling and food sufferers. The names reflected the gallows' humour that prevailed in HH.

The once luxurious carpet was now flattened and threaded, and the seating comprised faux chesterfields and the vinyl, high-backed chairs seen in hospitals and homes. There were a couple of old, well-used, squidgy draylon sofas most frequently taken by couples on the edge of boundary breaking.

Daria and Gary were slumped on one of these entre-nous sofas. Daria had moved closer to Gary as her disclosures got more and more intense. Gary could feel the warmth of her body, the outline of her hip against his leg and the touch of her arm as she gesticulated for emphasis. Her face was just a few centimetres from his as she continued,

"We are doing well, Gary, the business, it is good, and it is growing. This is my sixth rehab, and the towns before here are all now good customers. Every week, they want more than last week, every week family grows to make our business grow. Everyone in family does well from business but, you see, and you know, not everyone in family is family, some are like you, people we welcome into family, people who are safe with business and secret."

"And there was me thinking that you were talking to me because you want me to be your lover when really all you want is more staff," said Gary with mock ire.

"Perhaps it is both, Gary. What would you say then? What would you do if it was both, eh?"

"I'd be flattered and as excited as a teenager on his first date, but I see a problem here, Daria, in fact, I see a problem with you finding new family members in rehabs altogether."

"What problem? You tell me problem."

"Isn't it obvious? We are all addicts, except you, of course. I am an addict, and I would have thought that the last person you want to be involved in selling drugs would be an addict who might become his own best customer."

"It isn't so, Gary, not like that way at all with you. You are, er, Mr Pivo, Mr Cabalie red wine, Mr Soplica vodka. You do not do the shooting up, the snorting, the pills, the bong, you are not Mr Snowy or Mr Smack. You don't want family products. Food and wine, yes, but not other family goods, so you are safe, and you know addicts, how they work, how they need, you are good candidate for family member."

Gary looked at Daria without expression. She smiled a knowing smile.

"You make very good candidate for lover too, Gary. You can

be addicted to Daria; I know how to make you want more and more Daria."

"I can't think of anything I want more," replied Gary with a tremor in his voice, "but before our fantasy flies, I have to ask what you'll want from me, not as a lover obviously, I think I know that bit, but what you'll want me to do for the family business?"

"In small family business like ours, we do what is to be done. Sometimes we drive to airport or docks; sometimes we go to towns, we deliver, we collect, we manage, we give presents for good sales work, we punish for bad. Sometimes we make disappear. We all have to do what has to be done. We are family, not gangsters, not mobsters, but we have family law and family rules. If these broken, we execute sentence. Sometimes it is beating. Sometimes it is more. We do what we must do. You understand this, Gary?"

Gary understood very well. He had ruled over a similar regime of his own. Daria hadn't mentioned this part of his past, but he knew she knew. In the intimate confines of HH group therapy, where honesty is essential, Gary had revealed some of his nefarious past to his group members, one of whom was Daria.

8

"Ask any detective, and they'll tell you. Years of slog, months of grind, weeks of sleepless nights and what do you get? Nothing. Then, pow, all of a sudden, all those years, weeks and months rise up in line with Uranus and there are nuggets of gold hiding in the slag heaps slog. Guess what, Jo, go on guess what…"

Jo laughed. She was always amused by Max's boyish excitement when he was on a roll. She'd seen it when he brought in a new client. She'd seen it as he worked away to find solutions for knotty customer problems. She'd seen him relish working with new employees to help them become special and successful. Ever since his unfortunate dalliance with drug distribution, driven by Onetelcall's former CEO Spray Wilson, Dan had become a driving force for employee fulfilment and company achievement. Optimistic and irrepressible, Max had fought his way out from the dark to become, Jo thought, a beacon of light.

"OK, Max. I give in. I can't guess what, so why don't you tell me?"

"Oh Jo, Dan's going to be amazed. He'll be delighted, that's what!"

"Very good, Max, now, for God's sake, what's going on?"

"Ok Jo, Ok, it's this. You know we agreed that geography was the best way of using our available resources? If we focus on a most-likely region, we might come up lucky. Well, we have, Jo, we have!"

Max's tone and his news sent a shiver through Jo.

"Lucky as in hard work bearing fruit, you mean, what's the story then, Max?"

"I mean, it's not a full story yet, Jo. I don't want to over-egg it, but we limited our research and searches to Romania, Moldova and Western Ukraine as far east as Kharkiv and up into Belarus as for north as Minsk. It's a bloody massive area even so, but it is easy to break it down into activity hotspots. Gotta tell you, Jo, the activity in these regions is beyond any belief, there are farms and factories banging out emails, posts, videos, bent websites, copycat URLs, the whole gamut of cyber warfare is here, and it doesn't take as much digging as we thought it would to find at least the top layers."

"But we knew that from the word go, Max, didn't we?"

"In broad terms, yes, of course, we did; everyone does in reality, but what we didn't know was any specific cyber-gangster location. We couldn't trace IP addresses because emails, videos and posts all travel via hooky VPNs and bounce around so much, tracking them back to the source is, well, impossible."

"Yep, Max, that has undoubtedly been the case, but I know Dan and other teams in the Alliance have been trialling internet identity tracking with kind of reverse action mutations of super cookies and cross-site tracking with URL parameters. I don't fully understand what all that means, but I know they are optimistic in using these techniques against corporate cyber-thuggery."

"Yeah, well, whatever, but our breakthrough isn't nearly so complex or clever; it was, to be honest, a bit of a fluke. One of the team picked up on a food and wine company operating over there in the region and joined in on their social media pages; they are on Facebook, Twitter, Instagram and YouTube and so on, as well as some of the Russian sites like Odonklassniki and Vkontakte."

"What made- who is it, anyway? What made you look at this particular company?"

"Nothing tangible, it was that we thought- it was Sue Cox, by the way, who hit on it. We thought that we'd just pick random organisations in the region which had a higher-than-average social media presence, and which also featured email campaigns and the like, and this outfit was one of those selections."

"I see. Well done, Sue Cox. Is she one of ours or an Alliance blow-in?"

"No, she's a Onetelcall girl through and through, has been with us for four years and usually works on external digital security for our retail unit. I co-opted her for our Alliance forensic team because of her specialist retail knowledge and the enormous potential risk all retailers have, especially food stores, for ransom and extortion attacks. This particular company got her attention 'cos of its name, which she wouldn't have even spotted if it hadn't been for Indira; she works here with Sue, you must have seen her, long dark hair and amazing eyes..."

Jo made an expression of prudish disapproval at such a personal remark. Max smirked lasciviously.

"So, she, Indira that is, noticed this exporter from Chisinau - that's in Moldova you know - anyway, she noticed it was called something like Moldovanu Sammy Luchshiy, which, according to Indira who speaks some Russian because of her relations in Srinagar where, I believe, some Russian expressions get picked up from the Tajikistan border area- what was I saying? Oh yeah, this name she says means 'very best', that's the Sammy Luchshiy bit but, and this is the thing, she says that luchshiy is also slang in the Russian drug world. Anyway, she, Sue that is, didn't think much of it, to begin with until she got a bit of tracking and monitoring in place and noticed an abnormally high amount of traffic which didn't fit the usual profile of a food and wine exporter at all."

Jo interrupted, "Is this serious enough for us to get Dan in here now, do you think Max?"

"Let me run through what we've got, at least what we think we've got so far, Jo and then if you agree, we could make a short presentation of the facts, the processes and possible actions for Dan and the others in the Alliance. Is that ok?"

Jo nodded.

"Sue and Indira put all of our usual stuff into action, you know, dodgy cell number patterns from bulk call-outs, character, word and spelling discrepancies and common error and spotter bots and crawlers, IP and USP bounce travel indicators and so on; you know the score now Jo, and let the intel pile up. They got another lucky break only a few days into close monitoring. Oddly, it came from the feds, well not the police as such, but a troll and hate crime specialist agency working for the Met, and they had identified the mobile phones of what they thought were English soccer hate yobs dishing out race abuse to some of our black players. The agency concerned had been allowed to track back these revolting texts, from the players' phones and through the carriers, interestingly one of the major phone companies has a stake in the Moldovan mobile business too, and they got to the offenders who originally sent the messages. With me so far?"

Jo nodded again.

"Anyway, what this agency found out was that at least eighty per cent of the racial trolling assumed to be from the UK's so-called fans didn't come from the UK at all. No, it was from overseas and some of them emanated from mobile phone numbers associated with our food and wine exporters. How's that for a shocker then, eh?"

"You sure about this Max? I mean, are Sue and Indira certain that the number blocks are really down to the company they are watching? It's all a bit too much of a coincidence and slice of luck to be easily believed, isn't it?"

"Not at all Jo, not at all, take it from me, in fact, take it from Sue and Indira too, this is all pukka, and you can look at the files for yourself, there's no doubt, but the next shocker is even more of a shocker. Listen to this; you see, the Moldovanu outfit seems to communicate all of its business over Facebook and other common platforms. Product updates, special offers, discounts, recipes, provenances, well, all sorts of commercial stuff aimed at retailers, restaurants and the like, all get posted online on social media. Ok?"

"I'm turning into a nodding donkey here, Max," smiled Jo as she nodded yet again.

"Good-o, 'cos it gets more complex. The girls then put the rest of the forensic team onto this file and asked them to run their cross-checks against known parameters of numbers, IPs, URLs, ISPs and so on and so on," Max paused, his voice catching in his throat with excitement. "They overlayed some of their known drug traffic against some of the Moldovanu activity and spotted some commonality. At first, it didn't look to be enough to hang a hat on, but now there are more than just linguistic and character set anomalies, there are mobile numbers, admittedly a lot of burner stuff, nonetheless solid cell phone evidence that somewhere in the Moldovanu food and wine set-up is a major drug dealing business pushing dope to wherever they make legit deliveries. We've got 'em, Jo, we've only fucking got 'em!"

"That's brilliant, Max, absolutely bloody brilliant, and you're right, Dan will be amazed and astonished all in one. I expect we'll show the Alliance a thing or two too, and that's a great thing all round, can't be bad for business either. But Max, what's next? I mean, can we prove it and even if we can, who do we go to and what can we do to close them down? Of course, we've got that Alliance, and that includes the enforcement agencies around the world, but I'm just sure that somehow, whatever they do just isn't enough, justice just never gets served when the law is invoked, unless, of course, it is the US trying to extradite our hackers who blow holes in their security."

Max laughed at this irony. He knew that courts throughout the western world were lax and lenient when cybercrimes were being judged. Bringing eastern European hackers, trolls and thieves to any court would inevitably lead to all sorts of political pressures and liberal demands for freedom of speech, anti-capitalist, pro-hacker propaganda and probably legions of organised disrupter campaigns too.

"I know what you are saying, Jo, believe me, I do, and I've thought about it a lot but, I've got to say, I haven't really got anywhere. I mean, we are part of the Alliance, and we have to be seen to be squeaky clean, don't we? There's no room for grey hats in the Alliance's fight or Dan's original vision, so it's the legal process as we know it, or it's... well, what is it, I don't know."

"You don't and I don't, although I bet we have similar ideas of a more comeuppance variety for these vile people. I think we have to do what you suggested and put a report together and let Dan and the Alliance decide what should be done next."

"Ok Jo, you're the boss. I'll have all the info gathered from Sue, Indira and the team and prepare a report of everything we know and how we know it. I'll include all the other agencies and teams involved, and I think you and I should at least offer some ideas of how we can react with maximum effect," Max looked eager, tinged with a little rascality.

Jo nodded, this time with a knowing smile. She understood Dan's motivation for instigating the Alliance. They'd talked about it enough at work at home, in bed and on days off. She knew how committed Dan was to fighting the filthy world of trolls, hackers and criminals. He would be, she knew, proud and bullish when he presented the Moldovanu paper. She also knew her man was more, much more, than a keyboard fighter or a meeting room sayer of strong words. They had been through so much together in a previous fight against injustice. She had seen his steel, his determination and his immutable belief in the kind of justice such malevolent miscreants so deeply deserve.

A premonition told her that Dan would report to the Alliance, he would discuss the legal options available to them, and, in his heart and mind, he'd be planning a more exertive alternative. Following the premonition, came an inspiration that she knew Dan wouldn't like. Probably Max wouldn't like it either. She certainly didn't like it. Like it or not, Onetelcall still had a significant shareholding belonging to a faceless, unknown body somewhere in the Americas. The body was a family affair of massive wealth and power. Onetelcall's founder, Spray Wilson, had been funded by the family of a man simply known as Jimmy. When Dan, with Max's help, exposed a UK drug dealer called Sniff Taylor, the repercussions had been felt in the USA where

Spray went into hiding with Jimmy's cousin, the beautiful Margarita, and Jimmy also disappeared from view. Jo knew that Jimmy's family had a long and merciless reach and had been responsible for commissioning death hits.

Was this a time for firepower beyond the legal constraints of the courts? Would it be more effective in ridding the world of at least one more drug empire?

9

"You're a bloody good actress," said Gary to Daria after she had admitted to being a mole, "I can see how you'd get yourself referred; that's probably the easy bit, but how do you fool the counsellors, nurses and medicos?"

"Well, I do know a bit about being addict; some family not always strong to stay away from drugs and become addict. I do what they do and say what I think they say, and is enough. I do work given by counsellors and speak in group and therapy like addict and nobody suspect me. Anyway, who would be here unless having to?"

Gary had to agree. No one would volunteer to experience the HH regime unless their need was desperate. It was strict and punishing. Beneath the care and concern was a steel discipline and rigid adherence to the words and thoughts of the Big Book, the Alcoholics Anonymous bible. Honesty, Gary had been told, was a fundamental principle of rehabilitation in HH. In practice, he found it was a process of stripping addicts psychologically naked and then rebuilding them without, it was hoped, the demons that made them seek refuge in drink or substances. He listened to Daria's curt English speaking the words of an addict in group therapy.

"My head is washing machine; I am sick and tired of being sick and tired; I have lost all, I don't deserve this chance, rehab is bubble, not life…"

The more Gary wondered at Daria's skilled mendacity, the more he realised that she was, in truth, an addict of her own making. She was, he pondered, addicted to her life of deceit, of wielding family power, of spreading ruination and to revelling, as an interloper, in their anguish. Gary understood Daria; he too could and would savour the agony of addicts, even though he still faced the prospect of achieving his own deliverance. Seeing

Daria's mimicry of addiction suggested to Gary the possibility of aping recovery. In rehab, there is no right or wrong, no exam to be taken before release, no adjudication and no report. Gary was aware that he had to complete his twelve weeks at HH, give the illusion of a sincere recovery attempt, and show plausible sobriety to his mother.

He did his work; he wrote his fourth step and bared his soul with searing honesty of the most fraudulent kind. His peers were impressed by his learning, his knowledge of the Steps, the traditions and Bill's Story. Like Daria, he entered the spirit of HH recovery with a will and an enthusiasm that many addicts simply couldn't match. Everyone was sure that Gary would be one of the successes, that he would leave HH and live a clean and sober life of joy and fulfilment; everyone except his counsellor who could spot a rotter a mile away. Three people knew the lie: Gary, Daria and his counsellor.

Daily life in Harbour House began early with a seven-thirty group meeting followed by an hour for breakfast, half an hour to prepare for the day, and then a full timetable of lectures, group meetings, exercise, mealtimes, counsellor sessions and evening visitors, usually recovering addicts who shared their experience. There was a strict curfew with lights out at ten-thirty; any nocturnal fraternisation was taboo. The weekends were a little more relaxed. HH residents were allowed to go to town for Saturday afternoon; they had to stay in groups of three and HH planted spies at strategic areas close to pubs and known dealer spots.

The seaside town, always busy with tourists and happy fun-makers, was more of an uplift for Gary than any of the spiritual optimism doled out in therapy. He and Daria, along with Bob or Frank, an amiable old drunk who was both deaf and disinterested, as the necessary third person of the shopping party, had found a favourite café where they sipped large Americanos and nibbled shortbread; they always paid for Frank as a tacit appreciation of his natural discretion. Gary and Daria talked about their future with an adopted entre-nous lexicon to keep

Frank even more distant from their meaning than his deafness imposed. Food and wine needed no linguistic camouflage while drugs and pushing had to be expressed as ingredients and recipes; pushers became chefs and waiters. It was, they knew, a little puerile, but it gave them an intimacy of thought and purpose. In their plans over coffee and in quiet times at HH, Daria groomed a willing Gary for his new role in the family firm. An instinctive understanding of human motivation gave Daria an advantage in such mental preparation and commitment; she created in Gary an evident devotion, and she was confident in his loyalty.

Sunday afternoon was visitor time at Harbour House. Worried wives, anxious relatives, guilt-ridden parents and inquisitive children all piled into the commodious country house to speak in hushed platitudes, share hope if not expectation, exercise practised optimism, uninformed understanding, and eat lots of cake.

On the sixth afternoon of his twelve-week sentence, Gary, who had insisted that he wouldn't have visitors, was introduced by Daria to her uncle.

"Call me Alex," said Alexandru," shaking Gary's hand and smiling in a welcoming way as though he was hosting a family reunion. "Daria has written much about you to me. She writes a good letter, very descriptive. She tells me that you join the family company with her, very good, you are very welcome."

Alex asked various questions about his past interests and experiences, all of which Gary batted away with the ease of a test batsman facing the village eleven's second bowler. Gary was gifted with the art of plausible obfuscation. Alex was equally skilled at noting such traits and approved; dissembling was a required accomplishment for family business staff.

It was week ten when Alex appeared again. Gary could see that Daria was surprised to see him. They had been strolling through the grounds, as they usually did on Sunday afternoons to escape the applied smiles and sick-making pleasantries when Alex sloped towards them with the muscle-bound action of a former long-distance cyclist.

"Alex, er, uncle, why you here today, we had not arranged?"

For the first time, Gary saw uncertainty and possibly fear in Daria's eyes.

"We need to talk, Daria. You and me, we need to speak of family business. Gary, you don't mind? Not yet are you family business, so Daria and I will talk alone?"

"No, that's fine, I mean, of course. Tell you what, I'll leave you two alone and I'll pop off and get us a tray of tea and cakes; that'll take me about half an hour in this scrum, will that be ok?"

"Is very kind, Gary, half an hour is good enough for chat and tea with cake will be most welcome."

When Gary returned to the quiet spot in the garden where he had left Daria and the man she called uncle, he put down a tray of teas and cakes in front of two very sombre-looking food and wine exporters.

"Am I interrupting?" asked Gary, sensing the fretful atmosphere. "I can come back a bit later if you like?"

"Sit Gary," said Daria coldly, "we need you to sit and hear news, not good, you know, news not good and I want you hear it, you say what could be done."

Gary sat dutifully as directed and gave Alex his full attention.

"Family business, Gary, you know about family business from what Daria has told you, yes?"

Gary tipped his head in confirmation.

"We have a problem, a new problem we think. We are not sure yet, but we think it is a big problem."

Daria picked up the conversation, "Yes, Gary, family under threat here in UK. Before I tell more, I want you to convince Alex that you will be good family member too, how you want to join and work with us; then Alex will tell you problem and we see if you can help family and if family needs you."

Gary felt betrayed for a moment; something special between him and Daria had been violated by Alex's intrusion. In his rehab stupefaction, being denied alcohol and spoon-fed Librium didn't make for mental clarity, Gary had created a Bonnie and Clyde movie in his mind, with him and Daria fighting the world to become international masterminds of corruption and hard-hearted villainy. Now, he had to apply for the job Daria had included along with the role of lover and, befuddled though he might be, his instinct for survival-driven deception surged to the front of his mind. There was a little anger too, mixed with the delusory outrage of a spoiled child. His infatuation with Daria shrivelled as his indignation grew.

Fixing Alex with his best hard-man stare and pointedly ignoring Daria, Gary said, "Let me get this right Uncle Alex," he thought being deliberately diminishing with a hint of sarcasm would be a strong starting position, "your family business here is in a spot of bother, and you don't know where to go for help."

As Alex began to interrupt, Daria looked astonished at Gary's new attitude.

"No, don't stop me, I'm talking. You see, what I find here is a couple of people who have a disguise of respectability but are actually just common or garden criminals. I see a business that calls itself 'family' to make it somehow tough and intimidating like the real Mafia but, in reality, it isn't that at all; it peddles dope to people who can't say no. Hardly a tough-guy gig, is it? But now something's gone wrong, and you need either an injection of brain and resources to fight the threat, or you need a fall guy to tuck up and take the blame for whatever it is you reckon will help you wriggle from the hole you've got yourselves in. So, I'm not telling you why I want you to do me a favour, I'll tell you why you need me and what I need from you to make your family business of any interest to me." Gary's hubris gauge had just hit the red zone.

Daria looked flushed and obviously crestfallen. Her pet had shown her up and let her down, all in one go.

"Gary, you angry now, I'm not knowing why. You were wanting to be in family all the time we have spoken, and now, when family reaches to you, you change into little big man, starting fight before you know how strong is the person you fight with. Why, Gary? We are same people, you and me and Alex, we are same. You help us, we help you, that's how it is in family. Nobody tuck you up or make you fall guy. Ok? You want Alex tell you problem and you help family like we talk, or do you not want working with me when we get out of here?"

Gary looked at Daria as she implored him to soften his stance and his affected cockiness, his sense of being somehow undermined, abated. He smiled at her and nodded his acquiescence.

"Now, you and Daria have become team here in rehab, I think," said Alex with reduced assertion, "and Daria is essential, very, very important in the family. You'll do well in the family with Daria, make a shed-full of money and have very great power here in UK and all the places our family does business. I welcome you for all people in the family. I'll not ask you to tell me why the family should take you in, you'll not ask me to tell you what the family has to do to convince you of how big, strong and powerful the family is, it is so, yes?"

"It is so, Alex," replied Gary, "but we aren't going to get any further until you describe your problem, your threat or whatever it is that's rattled you."

"Daria has told, I think, of how the family uses online services like Facebook and all obvious, not secret ways to talk to each other?"

"She has, in some detail."

"Good. So, see, Gary, some of our conversations are real business, food and wine for customers in hotels, restaurants and so forth and so forth. That is good. It is as you say a smokescreen, to see messages that aren't real business you'd have to read thousands that are real."

"We call it hiding in plain sight," said Gary a little pointlessly.

"Hmm, whatever sort of hiding, it is good and works. Daria has told you we have governments asking us to do computing work too?"

"She has Alex, and I think I understand the full implications of the sort of work you do, we call it hacking and trolling, amongst many other terms. So, in short, you use social media platforms for legit communication in your family's business. You also use the same platforms to run and manage drug smuggling and pushing while, at the same time, you have a hacking, trolling factory which you use to extend your influence as a major drug player and which your government, or whoever uses to produce whatever disruptive, disingenuous, demotivating and downright dangerous disinformation they tell you to publish. Is that about it, Alex?"

Alex's face twitched into a frown of annoyance.

"Not us or the governments are as stupid as you think. You think of simple computer coding when we think of Esolang and Knuth. Behind open hiding is another layer of clever closed hiding, so governments and other customers with big points to make pay a lot to publish and not get found out for being the authorities behind their messages and posts. Don't think we are dumb, Gary, a big mistake."

"Ok, you're all very clever, and I'm sure you are by the way, but it doesn't change the fact that, as we speak, you've got a big problem and it doesn't take a genius to work out that you've been caught with your clever coding trousers down and someone is getting up your arse, right?"

"Well, yes Gary, that is it in nutshell, if you want to say it that way. Our people in offices in Chisinau have identified the actions of investigators. They see searches and accesses, some not the sort of access we see usually. They say it means someone is, as you say, getting up our arse and see our movements."

Gary sniggered, for a moment he was back in year seven.

"Not funny, Gary, serious. Very serious. So, listen Gary and think about what I say. Our people, whatever you say, are good. They will find out who spies on our services, we'll soon know who they are, what they are, where they are and why they do this. Then Gary, then you have a chance to do family work and earn your place by side of Daria in the business, you see?"

"Let me get this straight, you two," said Gary looking at Alex and Daria in turn, "am I right in thinking you want me to be a mister fixer for you? You want me to go after whoever is putting the eye on you and do something to stop them, is that what this is all about?"

"I told how it is in family, Gary," answered Daria. "I said what we all do, what we have to do to keep family business safe. No-one in family can be let-off from duty, you know what I'm saying?"

Gary looked around him. It seemed somehow quite bizarre. On a sunny Sunday afternoon, in the safe confines of Harbour House rehabilitation facility, in beautiful, tranquil, traditional English gardens, he was being propositioned to become a hitman.

10

Jo and Max had prepared their evidence with the punctilious professionalism of a Onetelcall new client pitch. Oddly for Jo, she felt, just then, as though her husband, the man she loved so much, was a sales prospect, someone to be persuaded, convinced and cajoled into an agreement to something she knew his automatic reaction would be rejection. The forensic team, working in Onetelcall in concert with the other Alliance troll and hacker action teams, had provided an extensive case file against the web brigades' cybercriminal factory and all of its traceable functions. It made darkly disconcerting reading.

In the early days of tracking, the team had identified, behind the happy talk of salata du boeuf and sarmale, of cognac-like five-year-old Golden Stork or Kvint, hid messages about deliveries and distribution of a more lethal variety, some coke, some 'real' heroin but, more terrifyingly and dangerous, mainly the flesh-rotting Krodakil, a Russian homemade heroin.

After Indira's sharp-eyed discovery of the illicit practices of Moldovanu Sammy Luchshiy, they had pattern-matched many of the drug-based online conversations and participants. As far as they could tell, there were two centres of operation emanating from Moldavanu's prodigious stock of nom-de-troll, IP addresses, cell numbers and identities. The activity masquerading as comestibles supplier and customer communication was all about cybercrime and trolling output.

Less political and with no attempt at social engineering, Centre One, as the team labelled it, specialised in extortion. They had identifiable activity in ransomware and encryption, spoofing, phishing and adware, zero-day threats and brute-force attacks, rootkits and rats. Centre Two, seemingly operating from the same geographical area and with the same sub-structures, was fanatically political, disruptive and havoc-targeted. The factory disgorged thousands upon thousands of posts, messages and comments in every shift.

Political upheaval and unrest, gender and gender identity forum infiltration, religious provocation and incitement, government and corporate imitation, fakery and misinformation, colour and ethnicity incendiary division, and the invasion of all forms of online social media, games and comment opportunities were massive and obviously determinedly seditious and abidingly undermining.

The team believed they had uncovered something significant. Here was a two-tier operation; one aimed at making money and selling drugs, the other was far more ominous and, they surmised, government-sponsored from the east or an eastern-Sino-Asian-Arab- rebel states axis or any other permutation thereof. This was hacktivism on a significant and evil scale. From its output, the team could make basic conclusions. From Onetelcall's previous experience and intelligence shared within the Alliance, the team's attempts at hacker and troll attribution had built a model of the enemy's practices.

Outrageous and effective, Centre Two of the Chisinau farm might be, sophisticated and esoteric as it might believe itself to be, it made some bloomers in its day-to-day outpourings of subversion and mendacity. In some cases, victim organisations, such as large companies and universities, had been able to backtrack their attacker using nothing more elementary than TCPView and Traceroute. The hacker's favourite search engine, Shodan, revealed suspect connections and devices in the region of interest.

Blunderingly, posts, comments and messages used identical syntax and linguistic and idiomatic errors. They posted within limited time slots, suggesting shift work and content tended to be hyper-targeted rather than the more general comment of most legitimate social media. They frequently block-messaged contentious hashtags with transparent re-writes of prescribed phraseology. It would be to Dan's ironic amusement that the greater the lengths the troll farm boys went to maintain anonymity, the more fissures for identity tracing they opened.

The case file that Jo and Max put before Dan provided unequivocal evidence that they had unearthed a major player in social media subversion and methodical, strategic crippling of western society and communities.

"This work is nothing short of brilliant," said Dan to a radiant Jo and an excited Max. "I knew Sue Cox would be an asset to the company but she, with, I must say, Indira's instincts and knowledge have come up trumps. The Alliance will be impressed; does Onetelcall a bit of good too."

"See what a wife can do for you, lover-boy?" smiled Jo, "and a good friend too," she added, glancing at Max. "The forensic team we've worked with has been an inspiration and they deserve an outcome of appropriate punishment of the criminals they have identified and reported."

"Couldn't agree more on all counts," replied Dan expansively. "I'll put this amazing case file to the Alliance and we'll discuss what our best course of action might be. Personally, I'd like to go over there with a machine gun and explain my views, our views, the old-fashioned wild west way, but I'm sure the Alliance will be more circumspect."

"Ah, well boss, that's the thing isn't it," said Max, his bullishness rising, "Jo and me, well we think that the Alliance will want to do, and be seen to be doing, what they will call the right thing. They'll want to go to the usual authorities, use the usual sanctions that the law allows and will end up not catching the crims, not identifying the powers behind the posts and effectively doing sweet f.a."

"I don't know about that, Max; I think there is a lot of power in the Alliance, certainly enough to close down the Chisinau operations and probably the Moldovanu outfit too, snake and head, Jo, as you always say, snake and heads."

"But Dan, isn't it you who always rattles on all the time about comeuppance, about holding people accountable, about punishments fitting crimes? Well, here's a world-class example of world-class crime and world-class cyber-thuggery, of world-class drug peddling and, come to that, a world-class killer of a drug which makes it even worse. Max and I don't believe that anything the Alliance can do, any laws they invoke, and action they take will be anywhere near enough the hammers of hell which should fall over the people behind this abomination of an organisation."

"Jo, darling, we can't go around righting wrongs like the bloody Lone Ranger. We are part of an alliance that has some of the most prominent international cyber-crime agencies, security companies, government bodies and IT leaders in the world as its members. I can't just waltz into a meeting and say, 'hey chaps, anyone got a six-shooter to get baddies with' now can I."

"Don't damn well dare be condescending and all darling with me Dan, you know better than that and, don't forget, I know these people better than you do; it was me who introduced you to some of them in the first place. I also know, from bitter experience, how you and Max feel about retribution. Do I have to remind you again of what you did to Sniff?"

"Another thing, boss," added Max, "and I don't want to sound hysterical or create danger when none exists, but it occurs to me that these people might not fight by the Queensbury rules, and we might already be in their crosshairs."

"What do you mean, Max?" asked Jo. "You haven't said anything about this before."

"No Jo, I haven't, and I might be scare-mongering with no good reason but, if I'm right like I usually am," he paused for collective harrumphing, "the bastards we have exposed will know that we have got into them, they will have all the intrusion alarms and tracker-tracer systems that we have; be sure they'll know who we are and where we are by know. They won't be happy, that's for sure."

"Max, that's not being alarmist, that's a bloody good thought, and we all know how up for a bit of murderous vendetta these eastern hoodlums and gangsters are. You have to be right, of course, they'll know they've been rumbled, and I'll bet they have got all that computer power protecting everything to the nth degree; their government or terrorist masters will make sure of that and they'll insist on being as hidden and safe as possible. If they've worked out who and where we are, which is child's play to them, there will be repercussions, and they won't be pretty, I suspect."

"Yes, well, Dan, I, that is we, have had a thought about that and you won't like it, you won't like it all, but you've got to listen; hear us out before you judge, ok?"

Dan swung his chair to gaze from his office window. He looked out over the car park and his mind went back to the frightening days of drugs coming into his company, of his old friend and chief executive and the family he got into bed with, literally and financially. He knew what Jo and Max had been discussing and he understood why they'd be reticent in suggesting it. He felt the inevitability of what was to come.

"Yes, Ok Jo, but before you leap in, let me remind you of something I think you'll find relevant to what you want to suggest." Dan gazed at Jo's surprised expression. He felt, yet again, the need to protect her. "Onetelcall has a big shareholder who isn't altogether a stranger to the drug world and its associated violence and unholy code of conduct. Follow me?"

"Oh yes, Dan," answered Max, "we follow, in fact, we were already there. Don't know, chum, how you read it, but I'm thinking that this Moldovanu mob will possibly know the people behind the shares, they might know of Onetelcall's... um... unfortunate shall we say, association with the drug world and being caught at it, so to speak, by a company which was funded by what is probably south American drug money, isn't going to sit too happily is it?"

"You're right, Max," concurred Dan, "when I started the Alliance fight against anonymous and loathsome trolling and hacking, I didn't for one moment think that we'd end up on both sides of the battle, but we are, aren't we? We ride the white horses of rectitude and righteousness but right behind us are the black horses of murderous, blood-sucking depravity; it's a bind, that's for sure."

It was Jo's turn to become the hawk. She arranged herself on the edge of a desk, pulled her ponytail back to maximum neatness, crossed her tight-fit jeaned legs and put her hands together, almost as in prayer.

"This is serious, possibly deadly serious, and I've been doing a lot of thinking about it. I haven't said anything before except for an outline of my thoughts with Max, and certainly, Dan, nothing at home, it just didn't seem right. But now it is right, and it has to be said, so here goes."

With another tug of the ponytail and a lick of the lips, Jo was ready for the most unusual and disquieting address she'd made since giving evidence after being attacked on her own doorstep.

"I'm not going to dress it up, ok? We have blood money owning our shares, and we know it. We know the people involved are every bit as bad and dangerous as any film characters make them out to be; they sell death and they kill in so many ways, from addiction to gunshots. We know it, don't we? We also know that we have, possibly a little blindly and with some self-delusion, trapped ourselves by our brilliance, hoist by our own petard is the expression, I think. We have pulled the tail of a fire-breathing demon and now it is probably out to burn us in our beds. So, to the left and to the right, we have murderers, and we are in the middle. So, my dearest men, I suggest we do some matchmaking; let's put our bad guys up against their bad guys and let them fight it out. That way, we might duck the being killed bit, which would be handy and both sides might inflict serious damage on each other, which is a sort of two-way requital. Each side might be each other's nemesis; it's almost poetic."

"That's all very well, Jo, but just how do you think…" Dan didn't get very far.

"Yes, Dan, I've thought about that too. Just how do we set

foe against foe? Well, first off is that we have no idea when the Moldovanu mobsters might decide to strike at us. And then, by the same token, we don't know if our American friends know or care about their eastern European counterparts or whether they have any appetite for such a distant fight, even if a company in which they have shares is a potential target.

"What we do know, or think we know anyway, is that a pretty robust form of violent retribution is likely to be coming our way and we'd be wise to engineer whatever precaution we can. I also think, and neither of you will like this, but I do think that once all this kicks off, Onetelcall will become damaged and tainted. Even if we survive, we won't have what we have now and we certainly won't be best mates with the Alliance crew.

"Sooo," Jo paused for another lip lick and hair tug, "what about this for a plan? How about we get hold of someone in the American shareholder firm or whatever they are and offer to sell them all the remaining shares at a rock-bottom price if they can weigh in and save both the company's reputation and the lives of their fellow shareholders? After all, without us, they have nothing and if the company gets caught up in an international drug, hacking and trolling outrage, it will be worth nothing too. They have, by our measure at least, a lot of money tied up in Onetelcall and our profits are now pretty significant, more than enough, I'd say, for them not want to lose."

She breathed out heavily, as though ridding herself of a great weight.

"I agree, Jo, in fact, I don't think we have many choices. If we are over-egging the danger, then we'll lose nothing; if it comes to some form of hideous war between hideous people, then we must do all we can to protect ourselves and, come to that, all those who could be caught up in the conflict, people like Sue and Indira, obviously."

"Cripes," said Max, "what a malarky, eh? Life's never dull with you two, is it?"

Dan and Jo looked at Max with affection and appreciation.

He had lifted a sombre mood and raised their spirits too.

"Sorry, Max," smiled Jo, "you didn't think you were signing up for all this when you joined the company, did you?"

"Actually, Jo, Dan, you know, I've feared that we'd not heard the last of the whole wretched drug world for a long time, that somehow it would come to a head again, I just knew it. And you know, I still feel so guilty and so much in debt to you two, to the company and all its wonderful staff and even to this town, Olderbury, and all the people who I may have, no matter how stupidly or remotely, harmed. I make amends like I have to, and I will keep on doing so, although it doesn't lift my guilt much, my need to protect you two is just as strong as it was during that terrible attack on Jo and all that followed.

"We agree, don't we, that Jo is onto what is possibly the only solution we have to a pretty knotty problem. If the company goes sideways, we must do all we can to distance ourselves from it; that way we might well have sufficient cred left to be able to start again, if you want to, that is. That means you'd both better do a bit of a disappearing act and leave it to me to sort out the Alliance and have a go at twisting the Americans into action. Don't forget that I was Spray's boy before the shit hit the fan. His chums might still think I'm kind of one of them, so I stand a good chance of making Jo's plan a reality."

"Of putting your head in a noose," said Dan, worried about his friend's proposal and chances of survival in trying to make it happen, "or a target on your back, you could be volunteering to be a dead man."

11

It was the custom in Harbour House to hold a celebration for each resident before they left after their twelve-week rehabilitation and hopefully the start of their long-term recovery. It was a residents-only event, with no counsellors or therapists, just the houseful of people who had been strangers and become friends, bonded in the way that those who are joined in adversity so often experience. Traditionally, such celebrations were just for one graduate, but Gary and Daria elected to hold a joint event as Daria had retimed her departure to coincide with the end of Gary's course of treatment. Of course, there was no champagne, just ginger beer, sparkling water, tea and coffee with cakes and nibbles supplied by HH's professional catering staff.

The structure of the evening was set by years of repetition. All the inmates sat around in a large circle in the main hall and the graduate, graduates, in this case, were given away by their buddies. Daria's buddy was Judith, a lost and desperate middle-aged woman on her third attempt at recovery in HH. Judith was sad and had found a strand of sympathy in the usually indurate Daria, who related to the woman's isolation from family and children, all of whom had now completely shunned her. Daria relied on the strength of her family and its associated honorary members and couldn't see how Judith could function without either her family or her beloved dry sherry. Nor could Judith.

Henry became a full-blooded Akintoye for the night. As a riposte to the non-stop ribbing he took about being an African chief and a tribal warrior, he had dressed in a homemade plumed headdress and stood bare-breasted with a leopard skin throw fashioned as a cut-down agbada. He also carried a broom handle with a cardboard spear attached. The HH crowd, where racism just didn't exist as all inmates, no matter their origin or inclination, joined together against their shared enemy, applauded

Henry with a raucous round of imitation war-like whoops and yells.

As the role demanded, Henry, in a parody of Akintoye, gave the eulogy. Gary was, he said, a good friend and a good man, in most respects, apart from his drinking and lust, of course. The audience loved it. Henry went on, in a mock-accented soliloquy, to describe a few funny occurrences from Gary's stay at HH, made much of his interpretation of boundaries as far as Daria was concerned and, with an air of lascivious double-entendre, sympathised with Daria for not choosing a real man with a real tan and real bed-power, instead of this pale, flaccid excuse.

Daria tried to blush but couldn't. Gary laughed a lot, not sure if Henry was being affectionate or haughtily disdainful. Everyone in turn then imitated sincerity and affected affection as they said nice things about the pair and wished them well. None of them believed Gary would stay sober, and most of them thought Daria was a sham anyway, although they couldn't know to what extent.

In the dark and quiet of his last night in his single bed in one of the men's shared bedrooms, Gary moithered about his time in HH, about what he'd learned and about his future with Daria and her family. For three months, he had been saturated in both the good and the bad. He had been to Narcotics Anonymous meetings on evening outings from Harbour House, where he'd seen pushers selling drugs, possibly supplied by Daria's organisation, plying their pernicious, poisonous wares to the wretched and vulnerable. He'd also seen visiting recovering addicts, invited into HH to share their experiences, and tell of work of amazing altruism and heroic acts of rescue and recovery.

His counsellor, whom he believed he had conned, had seen through him from the outset and had worked hard on imbuing him with the sense of honesty, conscience and self-approval so essential to long-term sobriety. He had done his work and studied the twelve steps and all associated reading. For the duration of his stay, Gary had rediscovered how to eat, sleep, and be an active, accepted participant in a small, confined society. For once, he wasn't an outsider looking in. He felt better, he didn't want to admit it, but he was beginning to understand how the HH regime might work and what an addict had to do to make recovery a realistic lifestyle.

Daria had remained untouched by the process. She wasn't, after all, an addict and had no regard for the overbearing virtue and appropriated probity of the whole recovery doctrine. It had been Gary's indifferent callousness that had interested her about him when they first met in the rehab residents' lounge. Their conversations with Alex, and Gary's apparent willingness to be complicit in acts of extreme illegality and depravity for her, convinced her that she had profiled him accurately, even though she had recently noticed sporadic outbreaks of humanity in him. She didn't worry about what she saw as HH's brainwashing methods, she had her own techniques for coercion and control. She would soon create the Gary she and her family needed, and Alex, she knew, would be a suitably rigorous and hard-hearted line boss. Any unwanted soft edges would soon be hardened.

When Alex collected them the next morning, Gary could feel the sway of the rehab bubble abate as the grand front gates became a receding memory. They drove to Alex's home some two hours away from the south coast retreat and, in that time, Alex detailed the extent of digital intrusion into the Chisinau computer facility and described the possible and probable implications and outcomes.

For some time, it seemed to Gary that Alex was talking in a foreign language of acronyms and buzzwords. For all Gary knew about computing, he was at a loss to understand the technicalities of Alex's summary.

"Not worry, Gary, you don't need all technicalities, you just need full picture of threat and danger family is going to need to fight," said Alex when Gary admitted his technical inadequacy. "When you know how bad it is, you will know we have to fight hard and stop these vrags," Alex almost spat the last word, which Gary later found out meant enemies. "We fight to keep food and wine, you think? No, you know truth as we talk about, you know we fight to keep big business, we make millions of dollars and we have people who won't let us stop because they have share of money and we have to give. We fight to keep government with us, they turn on us, we be their vrag, we die. No other possibility. We know what they do if secrets come out, they will put blame on us, they will make distance away from us like snakes and then they kill anyone who knows what they might tell to hurt government."

Gary leaned back and looked out of the car window. In rehab, it had seemed so straightforward and remote. He and Daria would be together, and together they would make money and live happily ever after. Now the chill wind of reality blew, and Gary realised that he was at the point of no escape. He'd gotten into tight corners before, but this was different. There would be no refuge with his mother if this went wrong, nowhere to escape, nobody to protect him.

In treatment, he had written a little and thought a lot about the ups and downs of his life. It had been his principle to be in control and stay that way, not to trust anyone and to have contingency plans for all and any foreseeable hazard or danger. He was, he knew, a player and an opportunist, a schemer and trickster, an impenitent user of anyone and everyone on whom he could prey.

Daria saw the distant look in his eyes.

"I understand, my lover. I know you think of danger, and you don't know if you are man enough for job family asks. You not alone, I am in danger, Alex too, we all have threat against us and many of family in UK, overseas and at home, we all have very big danger now. You think not your fight? You are right. Not your fight, it is Alex fight, family fight, Daria fight. You can leave us and go home, be back with your mother, be safe, or safer anyway. You be at home, you stay sober and then what my man, then what you do? More little crime, hurt more people and run away. Say that you not as bad as me and stay safe and sober and… and what? You be a nothing, a nobody; you die inside while I die outside. Then you drink again, your mother not save you next time, perhaps you die outside too."

Alex picked up on the theme, "Gary, listen to Alex, you want Daria, she want you. I like you and you are welcome in family; we have said all this. You think you can run, jump out of car now and be very well thank you. But isn't so, is it Gary? How you know you not already in danger? I can tell you these people, these spies who try to ruin us, they are more clever than just computers. They will have, as you say, intelligence on us all; they might know about you already, you and Daria. They will track us and know every movement. Perhaps run away not a choice. You not fight and you die, you fight and perhaps you not die. Is that how it is, Gary? I think that is how it must be."

In less than two hours, Gary was fully conditioned and programmed. Daria and Alex had closed their trap so persuasively that Gary felt relieved and grateful. He knew he would do anything for Daria and now he was pretty sure that anything it might have to be.

"You keep talking of killing and being killed," said Gary, now at one with his new family, "but we don't know who is going to kill us or who we have to kill to stay safe and keep the business going unscathed."

"Tonight, we meet geeks from home. They fly in to meet us and tell us all what we need to know and who is our target to stop more spies. You and Daria, you meet them and know who is enemy, who damages us and who we will have to stop."

There was a rented people carrier in the drive of Alex's old farmhouse in the northern part of Oxfordshire, Alex parked alongside it and the three went inside to meet the visitors. The four geeks had flown from Odessa to Sharm el-Sheikh and then on to London, looking like holidaymakers, they thought. Alex chuckled.

"You look like geeks pretending to be surfers, not fool anyone, pah!"

"Take no notice," said Daria, "is good to have precaution and make travel not obvious, you look very holiday," then she chuckled too.

The geeks adopted a synchronised sulk.

"We not fancy-dress spies, we just make journey look innocent. It is innocent anyway, we don't want trouble from nobody. Your cousins, they say pretend to be tourists, that what we do."

"Perhaps we should all introduce to Gary," said Daria. "Everyone, this Gary, he is joining family and will help with what you tell us, Gary this is…"

"Just call me Adeen," said the lead geek, "not my name, Russian for number one; we keep names secret from new people when not at home."

Lead geek went to each of his colleagues in turn, "This Dva, number two," Gary shook hands with Dva and moved to the next in line, "this Tree…"

"Don't tell me, that'll be number three then." Gary shook hands again and moved along the line. "And you'll be Chytirye, I expect," acknowledging the fourth geek.

"You speak Russian?" the lead geek looked wary.

"Not really," replied an amused Gary, "but being able to count and ask for a beer in most languages is a useful asset."

The geeks, uncomfortable in their sun shirts and shorts, disappeared to their rooms for an hour to change and wash the travel from their faces. Back in their obligatory satirical T-shirts and manufacturer-faded jeans and trainers, the geeks returned to the large old dining room and set up their laptops on the creaking old oak table.

"OK, my friends," said Alex warmly, taking control of the meeting, "we do not need a long introduction; we all know why we are here. Our colleagues from home, they spy on the people who spy on us, now they tell us what we need to know, please…" Alex indicated that the geeks should begin.

"OK, we notice unusual activity beyond our firewalls, our intrusion detection systems see unauthorised access attempts to our private network and looking at all our data for all our, er, business channels. I explain how we see this," said the lead geek, Adeen, as he opened a complex network incursion report on his laptop.

"Look here, old boy," interrupted Gary with an unintentional over-Englishness, "I'm sure you have chapter and verse about how your systems were breached and how you traced the intruders, but, for this meeting, we don't need all the details, just the headline facts. We need to know three simple things: who they are, where they are and what they know so far. Isn't that right, Alex?"

"Yes, for now, it is right, Gary," confirmed Alex authoritatively.

"It is right only for this meeting," asserted Daria, showing her authority too, "but if we are to go after spies on us, we must know how they did what they did. We may need this information when we track them down and deal with them. We may not, but we may, that is what it must be."

"OK," said Gary, heading off Alex's evident irritation, "I agree, the more we know technically, the better armed we will be, but, for now, let's just get to the nitty-gritty, shall we? I want to know who and what we, that is me, will be up against."

"What is gritty?" Geek Dva spoke up for the first time, looking confused.

"Ok," said the lead geek, "here is what we know. We have been totally hacked and cracked. Spies know all about old family business, about drugs and our friends in countries, but especially here in UK. Spies also see inside our farm; they see output and will know where it came from. They will guess government, but we think they not see any proof of government, just us posting content."

It was Gary's turn to get irritated, "Ok, ok, we get it, we know what's happened and that it is cataclysmic, but who the fuck has done it? Who has got to you, eh?"

"I am telling, let me speak," replied Adeen huffily, "no need for rude. I tell you we know original IP address, even though spying was routed all around servers everywhere we track it back to Olderbury in UK, where Onetelcall has HQ. It is them, Gary, it is Onetelcall, but we don't think they work alone, we think they have a team of helpers big in anti-hacking and security, and they must have some international agency support too to get all the information they need to get through our spoofing and break into our system."

"You know Olderbury Gary? You want to take your lover for dirty weekend there?" Daria looked at Gary; it was clear she didn't have smuttiness on her mind.

12

"The main problem with this scheme," said Max to Jo after their pivotal meeting with Dan, "is knowing where to start. I mean, Spray has gone into hiding in fear for his life, I imagine, and his buddy Jimmy has also done a disappearing act. I don't know how to get hold of either of them, even if they are still alive and can be contacted. We know, I suppose, the people acting for Spray's associates in the US and Mexico, and we could start with them, but they are all lawyers and accountants and won't, I don't think, tell us anything even if they could."

"Yes, Max," said Jo. "I'd thought about that too, but I don't think it's as big a problem as you do. I'll tell you why. I think that we get our brokers to approach the shareholders' representatives in both locations and offer them our shares at a giveaway price. They'll immediately smell a rat and come to us. I'd bet on it, in fact, I am betting on it."

"Dan, cool with that?"

"Yep, I broke my promise about not taking this mess home and ran through the scheme with him again last night and he agrees. It didn't make for a romantic evening for us newlyweds," she smiled, "but it had to be discussed in-depth and I also wanted to make sure that Dan- I do love him so much, you know - that Dan keeps his profile low as you suggested and he's happy to proxy us, you and me if you see what I mean, with the brokers so we can act on behalf of the company and our own shareholding."

"Christ, that's a big leap for Dan; brings it home, doesn't it, just how deep this hole we've dug for ourselves really is."

"Doesn't it indeed, anyway Max me boy, I've prepared a letter of instruction, my own fair hand, well, keyboard, so there are no leaks. Here it is, can you read it and sign it, like lighting the blue touch paper."

Jo handed her formal directive for the brokers to Max, who read it and co-signed it without demur.

"OK, I'm off to the post office to send this recorded," said Jo, "then I'm going to collect Dan and make up for our lousy evening."

Max winked.

At midday the next day, an expensive, exclusive London chauffeur-driven, dark-windowed Mercedes parked by Onetelcall's front doors and two very expensive suits, one male, one female, stepped out carefully, as though not wanting to tarnish their expensive shoes with parochial paving.

"Dandridge and Johnson, Carrington Hickman," the elegant man said with maximum asperity to the Onetelcall's entry system microphone.

"Jo," said the receptionist on the telephone, "I have a lot of names here for you. As far as I can make out, it is a Mr Dandridge and a Ms Johnson from a company called Carrington Hickman, but it could be the same names in a different order. The man is most insistent that he sees you and Max, and I quote, 'straightaway and without any waiting please'."

Jo giggled, "It is OK, they're from the city and don't live in the same world as the rest of us. Bring them up to the boardroom, will you? And get Max to come to my office first, please."

Max had seen the two visitors from his office window. "Talk about strutting your stuff," he chuckled as he walked into Jo's office, "they are living their created myths, those two."

"Brokers, Max, says it all, and before you say anything, she's way out of your league."

"You can be so cruel," grinned Max. "So how are we going to deal with this? We can guess what they are here to ask."

"Well, Max. I'd say we stick to a sensitively modified version of the truth. They'll have an appetite for such a big transaction, they'll want to know in some detail why we are selling out and they have some stock exchange formalities to explain, but I don't think we should tell them that it's a ruse to get their hitmen to face down some eastern European hitmen who's sabre we have rattled, Ok? At least the sale is realistic, eventually, so we aren't misleading them too much."

Jonathan Dandridge was, of course, every inch the city gent. Although only perhaps thirty-five or so, he had the fustiness of tradition and decorum under his thousand-pound suit. Janet Hickman was blond, slim, elegant and stylish. She was all the adjectives she hated while apparently striving to make true. Janet hated her forename, hated assumed male superiority, hated right-wing traditionalists and harboured a misandrist bias, all of which was unfortunate for a woman in her role and with her rampant ambition and avarice.

Regarding Jo and Max with a cold, dismissive gaze, Janet took the lead, "We have received your letter. You must know we can't take an instruction such as this simply by letter, naive really to think we might. However, we can act for you after we have gone through the requisite protocols and necessities."

Visibly bristling, Jo was beaten to a response by the observant and protective Max, "Thank you, Janet, for your introduction, perhaps you could consider our letter to you as less an instruction and more a summons, and we thank you for responding so promptly."

Jo almost applauded; Janet looked slightly redder.

Jonathan took over, "We have no end of regulation forms and declarations for you to read and sign before we can even make our first move. Before all that, though, please indulge me by explaining why you, as key executives and such excellent performers in your field, want to offer your shares for sale to an existing major shareholder. As far as we can see, the company is exceeding all financial predictions and targets and, theoretically at least, we cannot sell your shares to a co-shareholder at a price not available to other, albeit smaller, shareholders."

"I understand all that, Jonathan," said Jo, "and I am very aware that our request causes all sorts of professional problems for you. The truth of the matter is that we are reaching the end of our Onetelcall lollipops. Dan and I recently got married, you know, and we want to have a life which isn't all work, all about the company and Max fancies paddling his own canoe and wants to realise some cash from his shares and be free of any restrictions which Onetelcall might otherwise place on him. So, you see we have very good reasons for wanting to sell the shares. To us, it makes sense that the other large shareholders, the people who put up the foundation funding, should be able to buy our shares in the company they started at a reasonable price, perhaps below market value but a justifiable price for them and enough for us nonetheless."

Mollified, the two brokers agreed to continue the process and spent another two hours of what Jo and Max thought to be sheer regulatory tedium.

"Bloody hell, Jo," said Max as the city couple were driven away, "that was a whirl of death, wasn't it? If that's what you have to do to earn their sort of city money, I'd rather stay in IT, thank you very much."

"Yeah, and I'm not sure they recognise the basics of customer and supplier. Do we actually have to have their approval to sell our own shares? I think we deserve a drink; let's get Dan and escape for an early supper."

Over a pizza and a glass or two of Orvieto, Max and Jo relayed the salient points of the broker meeting. They explained that they had agreed to the next action which would be for the brokers to write to their counterparts in America to make the offer of sale and provide some positioning for the decisions behind it.

"Right," said Dan, "it should do the trick. I can't see cynical American mobsters falling for our story about wanting a quiet life, they'll smell a rat for sure and I reckon we'll hear more from them pretty soon; I bloody well hope so anyway, otherwise, we'll have to think of a more powerful ruse won't we."

It was just three days later when another luxury car with tinted windows made a film-star-style tyre-squeaking entrance to Onetelcall's car park.

"I've come to see Dan Rackham, Jo Hadge and Max Golby. I don't have an appointment but tell 'em Spray Wilson's uncle is here to see 'em please, ma'am."

"Dan," Jo almost shouted over the internal phone, "it's worked, oh, my love, it's worked, we've flushed out one of Spray's er, relations, and he's here, he's here in reception right now. Crikey Dan, we might have a chance, after all; let's hope we can enlist them to help us. So, go home now while Max is in the meeting room. I'm going home too. We must stick to our plan and let Max take the lead now. Let's leave separately so nobody notices; see you at home lover-boy. I'll brief Max now and he can come over to us when he's finished with the man from Mexico."

Max's bravura had always been one of his most reliable assets when dealing with tricky meetings and it didn't let him down. He had rehearsed mentally for this meeting, should it ever happen, hundreds of times, and when he strode into the meeting room, he was confident in his purpose behind the share sale ploy.

The man from Mexico wasn't at all what Max had expected. He wasn't Mexican and he didn't look at all like a gun-wielding, drug gangster hoodlum. He was pale, slight and casually dressed in a checked shirt and chinos. His mousy hair was parted to one side and his features looked timid and deferential.

God, I hope we don't have to rely on him for salvation, thought Max as he held out a hand of greeting.

"Max Golby, welcome to Onetelcall and Olderbury. I am deputed to act for Jo and Dan and to do anything I can to help you and make your time with us as pleasant and easy as possible."

"Arthur Pincher, call me Art," replied the small man in a quiet, thin voice with a New York nasal undertone, "I'm here on behalf of your co-shareholders, following a letter we just received from brokers Carrington Hickman. Thank you for your kind welcome, sir, or may I call you Max?"

There was coffee and small talk for half an hour, during which time Max learned that Art was an east coast lawyer, retained by the consortium which collectively owned the existing Onetelcall shares in a convoluted financial structure of nominees and errant beneficiaries. Max could see that Art, unusually diffident for an east coast American legal consultant, was summoning the courage to make a proclamation and eventually it came.

"You see, Max, the thing of it is, well, let me say, that my clients, that is your co-shareholders, are well, how can I put it, sceptical about the motivations behind your sudden and seemingly too-tempting offer to sell your shares in what is, and I must say this with all honesty, a fantastically successful multi-nation company that can only keep on growing and make more profits. So, you see, they have, er yes, they have tasked me with asking you candidly, honestly and openly, hiding nothing and disclosing everything relevant, exactly why this offering is being made and exactly what is really behind it… and, may I say, Sir, er Max, I wouldn't recommend you attempt any chicanery or duplicity with my clients, they are not known for their forbearance or clemency when they feel slighted if you see what I mean? So, I do, I really do urge you to tell it like it is because it won't work well if my clients find you are trying to take them for a ride, not, sir, er Max, that I'm suggesting for a moment that you and your friends are anything but souls of probity and integrity. However, I must point out that they take into consideration your previous relationship, especially yours Mr Max Golby, with Ray Wilson, former CEO and founder of this company and now hiding away in exile, and my clients would point out that there are always questions to ask about motive with you in view of your history."

Art, brow now shining with perspiration, sighed in relief and looked forlornly at Max as a child about to be told off.

Max gave him his best reassuring smile and said, "Art, this

isn't easy for either of us, so let's make it a bit more relaxed, shall we? You've had a long day already and it isn't over yet because I've got a story I must tell you. How about we get out of the office? I'll take you to a lovely old English pub where we can have something to eat and I'll buy you a pint of English beer, you won't like the first one, but you'll love the third, how does that sound?"

Art let the tension slide from his shoulders, the pressure eased in his head and a sense of relief flooded through him.

"That sounds just fine Max, thank you so much. You're right, this is hard. I'm not a tough guy or a hard-nosed criminal lawyer. I deal in financial affairs, I'm spreadsheets and regulations, not crime and punishment, so this is all a bit foreign to me. But I do know my clients and I know that what I've told you about them is true, every bit and worse. To be honest, I'm not comfortable with all this but I do as my company dictates and as my clients bid, so I do thank you for making this easier and something to eat and drink, away from an office or airport, would be more than welcome."

Max and Art went to The Jackdaw, a gastropub in a picturesque village, much favoured by pre-Covid American tourists. It had struggled to survive during the height of the pandemic. After two years of enforced low-level trading and fill-in home deliveries, the pub had reformed in a Covid-tolerant way, with distanced tables and electronic ordering and paying systems. Max thought it had evolved for the better; it was more open, airy and discreet.

They had a late lunch of pork belly, crumbled black pudding, apple sauce and soft fondant potatoes, with pints of local bitter. English gastropub food was reliable and good at the Jackdaw, and Art ate with a heartiness which defied his slight size. He found the beer quite palatable and, after the second pint, felt a warmth and relaxation, which was welcome, given his mission.

Max took his time and recognised the moment to turn a potential adversary into an ally in a battle he didn't understand.

As Art leaned back, his meal eaten, Max started his play.

"What you were saying back in the office about your clients not liking being crossed, I can understand that. I knew Spray, Ray Wilson as you'd know him, quite well. I saw first-hand a hint of what he and his, ah, associates could and would do to anyone who broke their rules, so I know you aren't spinning me a yarn and I imagine you've been put in a position you don't relish?"

Art spread his hands wide in a 'what can I tell ya' gesticulation.

"It's my guess, Art, that you've been sent here with a hard and fast agenda, and, I think, it's more than just fact-finding, and more than getting to whatever motives there are for our share offer now. I'd bet you've been briefed with an altogether more arduous task. You've been told to make us do something, I don't know what, but something we wouldn't want to do in exchange for something we want. Right?"

"Ok, Max, I'll say this, no one can hear us here, so I can say openly that my prime objective is to get to the truth, just like I said. The fam... er... my clients, well they don't give two shits about what matters to you and your colleagues, they only want what they want. They want your company under their control, more than what they have now with the imbalance of shareholding, so on the face of it, your offer is an answer to a maiden's prayer for them. That's why they are suspicious, see?"

"So, what if they get what they want, what's the problem, just pick up our offer and bob's their uncle, surely?"

"Well, no, Max, if it were only that simple. You see, they want the company, that's the easy bit, but they need you all in place as respectable and trusted public faces at the head of what they want to do with the company if you follow me."

"And what do they want to do Art? What is it that needs us to stay as figureheads while the company does things which, presumably, we wouldn't necessarily approve of?"

"They want to use Onetelcall as a front for their new plan,

and I'll tell you what I know, so you don't have to push me anymore. What it is, what they plan is to fire up a European-based, you know," Art looked uncomfortable, "well, a communication system that nobody can ever trace. They have been looking at how terrorists work, like the Jihadists and like so many other influencers, they'd like to mimic that model for their particular purposes."

Max almost laughed at the irony; only Art's stressed, anxious expression prevented him.

"Let me get this straight, Art. You're telling me that you, that is your clients, want Onetelcall to become a troll farm, a hacking factory, a web brigade, is that it, Art, is that really it?"

"You'll hear no more from me, Max. I've said enough, I told you what you need to know, and I'll go no further. I have a responsibility, like it or not, to my clients and I've already pushed that boundary."

"Tell me this then, Art, what happens to you if you go home having failed in your mission? Your clients don't take kindly to their orders not being carried out to the full, do they? So, what do you suppose they'll say or do to you if we tell them to get stuffed?"

The warm beer turned to ice; Art's face paled again. He had heard of how lawyers in his line had disappeared before and he knew, if he went back to his clients empty-handed, he might join the ranks of the missing.

Max saw the consternation on his new friend's face.

"Tell you what, Art, don't look so panicked, I might just have a suggestion which can save both of our hides and it doesn't mean you have to give up on your professional obligations, although you might have to be more hand-in-glove with us than a lawyer would normally be with a client's object of action, how does that sound?"

Art felt like he was walking back down the steps from the gallows.

"You're going to love this, Art," smiled Max. "It's all something of a paradox because what your clients want Onetelcall to become is exactly why we want to get out of the company. Let me tell you what's been happening."

Over another pint of bitter and an exemplary cheeseboard, Max gave Art a carefully edited version, leaving out any reference to the Alliance, of how a team within Onetelcall had stumbled across proof of an eastern European facility which was behind an international programme of drug dealing, hacking and trolling on a mighty scale, and probably, with some foreign power state backing. He explained that it was not just probable, but certain, that Onetelcall's intrusions and probing had not gone undetected and that reprisals of the sort only mobsters and Art's clients would understand or order.

"We don't know for sure, but we believe someone, somewhere, will very possibly be thinking about sending a hit team out after us as we speak. You know I'm speaking the truth here, Art, that's why we want to cash in our assets for whatever we can get, distance ourselves from the company and hide away from any crosshairs for as long as it takes."

"You've got that right, Max; you're sitting ducks with fuckin' great targets pinned to your butts."

Art was evidently relaxing again and letting his professional guard drop a little. Max went for part two of his plan.

"But that gives you and me both a big problem, doesn't it, Art, because if we do a runner, with or without the shares being sold, the company still won't be available for your clients to do what they want to do and, as you said, they aren't easily thwarted. If we go and the company loses its board and, if I may say, its brains, your clients are well thwarted and you will, in their eyes, have failed, and we won't escape like we need to. It's a dilemma for both of us for sure, but not one without a solution, ready for this Art?"

Frying pans and fires crossed Art's mind, but he inclined his head in affirmation.

"Romanians, Moldovans, Russians, whoever they are, they know a thing or two about killing," said Max. "Christ, they try it on in suburban cafes here, and we have no way of protecting ourselves and certainly no way of fighting back. We are in mindless revenge territory here. Killing us won't now stop the exposure of their online terrorism but they'll do it anyway; it's the way of the world these days. So, Art," Max leaned forward with almost filial concern, "I suggest we wriggle out of this with our lives intact by you telling your clients that if they want what they want, they'll have to defend it and fight for it. Their assassins versus the eastern murderers; sounds like a baseball match."

Art, now four pints down and even though a little slower from his indulgence, was still quicker than most and he saw Max's strategy quickly and clearly. He looked at the Englishman with approval and near affection.

"That's smart, even by a New York lawyer's standards, that's smart. It gets me off the hook, and that's good, I can tell you, and I'm pretty sure I can sell it. You've never heard this from me, but I know where the top family man is. He went into hiding at the same time as Ray Wilson and a girl called Margarita, who ran off with Ray. My man, his name is Jimmy, a buddy of Ray's, wouldn't sacrifice him and had to disappear too, but I know where he is because he's still running the show. If he were Italian, he'd still be capo di tutti or whatever they say in the films. Yeah, I reckon I could fly this, especially as my neck is on the line too. The trouble with your scheme, though Max, is that it doesn't do too much to assure your longevity. You may be hit before our lot can act, you may be hit anyway, you may be hit even afterwards, there's a lot of thugs-for-hire and brainwashed fanatical psychopaths about, you know."

"Yeah, well, there's not a lot I can do about that, but I have had another thought. I'm sure you can convince your clients that they have to fight for what is theirs, for what they want, but once they've fought and won, they still won't have it all, will they? They won't have the dream team they need still at the head of their specious trolling empire, will they?"

Art's spirits went down the snake next to the ladder they had just climbed.

"True enough, don't suppose you have an answer for that too, do you?"

"Well, actually," said Max, believing now that he'd sown his seeds well, "I do, but it comes with caveats."

"Ok, lay it on me."

Max had done much soul-searching before this meeting and in preparation for just such an eventuality. He had never come to terms with his former miscreance; how greed and immorality had led him into aiding, abetting and enabling drug dealing. He'd tried to make amends. He'd given a lot of money away to rehabs, like Harbour House on the south coast, and to local addiction charities, but none of this absolved him in his mind from grinding guilt. Now was his chance to restore himself, perhaps not in everyone's eyes, but in his own at least and, to Max, that was what mattered.

"Here's the deal. Dan and Jo go now, tomorrow, immediately. Whatever happens, they are immured from any danger as of right now. That, Art, is a given; it has to be."

Art nodded in a 'go-on' way.

"This might play well with your clients because they know just how honest and upright those two are and how impossible it would be for them to bend to the family's heinous plans. Now, I, on the other hand, have a history with your clients, through Spray, which will make them believe that I am just the man for the job, and in many ways, I am just that. I am known to be venal, I'm better than most hackers in the dark art and I can put together a new team of young code cowboys who, for the right incentives, from social outrage to coke to money, will bang out any post to any platform with any message with one hand while the other breaks into the Bank of England's paying account."

Art was mystified. A man he believed could be a real friend had revealed he'd be happy to hop back over to the wrong side of the fence and help an organisation of mobsters fight another organisation of mobsters to create a new organisation for mobsters.

"Look here, Max, I understand that you're in a jam, a real tight spot and that you've talked me into trying to get my clients to go to war with people who want to kill you and your cohort. That I get. But why, Max, why are you volunteering to get back into bed with these people? It doesn't make any sense; you could be away free and clear."

"It does, I'm afraid it makes very good sense, and you know it. I've got the least to lose here and, in some ways, it's all my fault any of this is happening in the first place. Your clients won't accept the company without at least one of us left there to do what they want and keep the business looking legit. If they don't have that, they may not fight. Even though they are big shareholders, they may decide that this business just isn't worth the hassle, especially if the top team isn't there to make it happen as it has. If they don't fight, Jo, Dan and probably me, we might die. The only way to ensure they ride over the hill to rescue us is by thinking that they are getting all they want and that, given their grandiose plans, will make it worth fighting for. You know I'm right Art. Doesn't mean I'm a bad guy, just expedient."

13

The Royal George was Olderbury's highest-starred hotel; it showed four stars, without specific attribution, on its website. It held itself in high regard but sold rooms for the afternoon to expensively dressed executives and their high-heeled guests. Its waiters served main courses with synchronised cloche-lifting to reveal costly meals, the ingredients for which came from the local cash and carry.

Gary and Daria were not concerned with its pretension nor its food provenance. They needed a comfortable base from which to execute their crucial assignment, which was to find and stop the threat to their online activities. Alex and his four geeks had equipped Gary and Daria with a complete dossier, findings from all the tracing, anti-intrusion and online detective work. They needed little of this information. All they used was a company name, Onetelcall. It would be up to their detective work to find their specific targets, the people who had been responsible for spying on them.

"We could just fire-bomb the whole building," Gary had suggested enthusiastically to Alex before they left his farmhouse.

"We could not fire-bomb anything Gary, it is not family way. We do not cause big incident; it is bad to attract too much attention with big explosions or hurt people. What we do is not way of stupid guerrilla bandits. We are more clever in all what we do and, Gary, we must be more clever here too. You and Daria have simple job, and you not go beyond orders. You find people who made spying, know their names, know their faces, know what jobs they do, know about them. You find out who is giving orders to these people. Then you act, but not with fire or bombs. You use brains; now that you not drink, you can think clear and that is what you have to do."

Sitting in their family suite, one double bed and two single beds in one large room, Gary mulled over the options of their task.

"Why can't we just pop 'em off, eh Daria?" Gary couldn't believe he was sitting in a hotel discussing murder with a lover, but he was and now he was in so deep, he found the role surprisingly natural.

"You heard Alex, we follow orders, we do what is best for family and what family ask of us, they know best, that is how…"

"Yeah, yeah, that is how it is in your country, I know, but they aren't making it easy for us, are they? I mean, we have to find the top players and arrange for them to have an accident and then we have to identify the hackers, nobble them with threats, and make them so afraid they'll probably never sleep again. Sounds ok when you say it quickly but, all in all, it is a big ask."

"It is what has to be done, my lover. You and I fight not only for family but for us too. We do this right, we stay together, we become more powerful, we have big life ahead; that's what we want. If not what you want, you say now, but I know it is what you want deep down, so we make it happen, together, we can do it, we have to do it."

They had a good deal of research to do, and they had to do it covertly and discreetly. They hired a car, not from Olderbury's only car rental company but from a national agency in a neighbouring town some ten miles away. They had agreed to cover as many trails as possible and to wear their face masks everywhere they went, just in case anything went wrong to subject them to being hunted by the authorities. They had not considered that there would be any opposition from the target company or people.

They had, in their dossier, profiles of Onetelcall's most senior executives, and they identified Dan Rackham, the chairman and Max Golby, the CEO, as being the most likely joint candidates for their hit. After that, they were less clear as neither the dossier nor the four geeks' research had shone much light on who the spying staff might be. The geeks had trawled multiple professional networking websites and identified several people with relevant experience for cyber-security scrutiny. The list was longer than Gary and Daria would have liked; it had over a dozen names, including Sue Cox and Indira Bhatt.

From their hired small Ford, parked by a tranquil village green, the couple looked at the home of Mr and Mrs Rackham through their binoculars. They could see that no one was at home and they decided to prowl about. The old village property was conjoined at one end to another dwelling; Gary deduced that the properties were connected some time ago, probably as a pub or shop and a storeroom or warehouse. Both houses had been extensively renovated to combine postcard old English looks with modern living and luxury.

"What are we looking for?" Daria crept up the gravel drive, trying not to make a crunch, although why she was making such an effort wasn't obvious to her, it just seemed right.

"Anything that looks like a hazard or an accident waiting to happen, I suppose," replied Gary, "I don't know, we are playing it by ear at the mo, aren't we? But if there is to be an accident, it could be here, couldn't it? Although we'd only get one of them and might take his wife out too, we'd still have to deal with the other chap."

They let themselves into the back garden, through an unlocked side gate, and saw a compact, well-kept village house garden with a lawn, some flower beds, a hedge at the bottom of the garden and a wooden shed. Nothing looked like a lurking death opportunity waiting for a victim to their amateur eyes.

"Come on, Daria, there's nothing much to see here but at least we know where he lives. It's a start, I suppose. Let's get back to the car and have a dekko at the other bloke's place."

Max had stayed in the bachelor apartment he took when he first moved to Olderbury. It was part of a converted farm building and Max had tricked it up with all the tech he could find, originally for streamlined seduction and later for security and safety.

Gary parked in the shade of an old timber and brick barn. There was nobody about as they got out; Daria perched on the car's bonnet, took off her mask and enjoyed the feeling of the sun on her face.

"There's not much to see here, Gary, it's a flat over there," Daria pointed at the extensive farm building which now housed four attractive flats.

"Well, his car isn't here, and I don't think anyone is at home in any of the flats," replied Gary, also sunning his face, "I'll go for a wander, just to see if anything springs to mind."

"I don't think that tragic accidents at home are going to be our best bet, my lovely," said Gary, eventually. "I reckon their cars might be more useful, you know, brake pipes and that sort of thing."

"You know how this is done? You know how to fix car for accident? You mechanic Gary?"

"Alright, lover, alright, I was just thinking out loud. Actually, I do know a man who could fix the cars for us, without any doubt, but I don't think we want to invite anyone else to our party, do we?"

"Absolutely not, we not want stranger we don't know. Might not be able to trust such man. We do whatever we do ourselves and I think now that what we do is shoot and hide body, they disappear, like home, that's how it is…"

"…in my country," Gary mimicked.

"You take piss, brave boy? You make fun of Daria, you pay price in pain." Daria leapt towards Gary and clutched his crotch. She heard him catch his breath as she eased her grip and moved her hand slowly back and forth; she saw his eyes close and mouth open. She moved her hand more aggressively, with that blend of pain and pleasure which she knew he frantically wanted. He'd do what he had to do, she knew.

Gary playfully bundled Daria back into the car and drove

back to the hotel at full tilt. The receptionists sniggered knowingly as the couple scurried past them. The lift was at the top of the building, so the two lovers jumped up the stairs and just made it to their room before their clothes started to come off.

Excited and oddly exhilarated, Gary and Daria ordered room service. An embarrassed young waiter delivered burgers, chips, and two bottles of house red. Daria believed in the restorative power of red meat and red wine; her lover wasn't finished yet. Gary's post-rehab sobriety resolve dissolved in his surge of Rioja-fuelled lust.

The morning bought with it a couple of dry throats and heavy heads.

"We not able to have morning off now, Gary," said Daria after her second orange juice, "we work, we have not time to lose, family will be expecting report, I must call Alex."

Daria gave Alex an edited resume of their activities since arriving in Olderbury and detailed their inspection of the two top-of-the-list targets' homes. She explained that no opportunity for accidents was immediately apparent, and he concurred.

"A home accident is not the solution here Daria, too messy, too dangerous and could go wrong easily. I agree about what you say about car fixing too, we don't want no strangers involved now and a person who doesn't know how will not make for a good accident, not make for damage that police will not see easily. You must find another way, like you say, as long as bodies do not show up too soon, people will think they just run away, but what about wife eh Daria, she won't go along with the running away story, perhaps you might have to deal with her too?"

"Maybe, maybe not, we see what happens, Alex. We have list of people who might be the technical spies, I sent to you over our network."

"Yeah, I saw and I've got geeks to do more checks. There

were thirteen names on list, they have taken off seven of those, they explain why but I'm not able to explain to you, but of six names left, two of the females look most likely, they are Cox and Bhatt, see if you can find more about these, ok? Geeks, they find pictures of girls from social media. I send to your phone and to Gary too."

"Yes, Alex, send us photographs and we find out all about them; I call you later."

"Find out more about girls on list, Cox and Bhatt, he says, so we will. Where do girls who work at Onetelcall go, do you think? Do they go to pub for lunch, do they go to gymnasium, perhaps to shops, do they go together, we find out, come on Gary. Is getting to be late morning already and we must find out what we need and report to Alex; the family will be expecting results very soon."

"OK, my girl," said Gary, "let's check out the gyms first and then perhaps the pubs closest to their office."

They found five fitness centres in Olderbury and started with the most expensive. Daria volunteered to go in, armed with a photo of the two targets and with a cover story of looking for old friends from uni. They tried three gyms but had no joy. After the third, the effects of the previous night's excesses and as the time moved on to nearly one o'clock, they decided to head to the most likely pub and have a restorative lunch.

The closest pub to Onetelcall, only half a mile from the business park, towards the centre of town, was The Carpenters Arms. The pub had been recently refurbished and restyled to appeal to its new younger and more demanding customers from the offices springing up near them. It had once been the town boozer, run by a recalcitrant landlord and his ungracious wife. After the couple had been found guilty of all sorts of offences connected with town violence, drug dealing and other crimes, the brewery had taken it back under its control. A lot of money was spent on design and marketing, resulting in the faux-vintage, stylised restaurant and bar.

Gary walked to the bar while Daria chose a seat, giving her a view of the door and most of the drinking area. Gary had already failed in his bid to stop drinking as numerous glasses of Stallion red wine demonstrated, but old tricks crossed his mind in this first bar experience since Harbour House. Could he have an innocent tonic water with several shots of vodka hidden under the lemon? He could, of course, but who would he be kidding? It was his natural inclination to be devious, but he knew Daria would see through him. Would she care? Anyway, he'd been to rehab and was better now. He could control his drinking again; of course, he could.

He ordered two large glasses of Hungarian house red, it being both potent and closer to Daria's home and taste. Gary showed his mobile phone pictures of Sue and Indira to the barman.

"We," indicating a reassuringly smiling Daria, "are looking for two old uni mates of my girlfriend. She hasn't seen them for a few years now, you see, and she'd love to find them. They work somewhere in Olderbury, we think. Have you seen either of them? Do they come in here at all?"

The barman peered at the screen, "Oh yeah, I know them, but only 'cos they was in here only the other day, we were quiet and they spent a bit, that's why I remember. Came in with some smooth dude and another woman, a bit older than them, fit though."

Composed and confident in his mini-role, Gary turned to Daria and gave her a thumbs-up, 'He knows them,' he mouthed across the room.

Daria rushed to the bar with the air of someone finding their lost puppy.

"Oh, so grateful, thank you, you know these lovely people, my friends, how wonderful, do they come here again, you think? You know how I can contact?"

The barman gazed at Daria with ill-concealed boyish randiness. Gary wasn't alone in recalling old habits. Daria blushed seductively, but with Gary by her side, she moderated her response. The young barman wouldn't be worth turning over anyway; his credit cards would be maxed out, no doubt.

"No, they don't come in here much, well, if at all actually, apart from their session the other day, celebration I reckon but I don't know what, a birthday, or promotion perhaps. But I can help you 'cos I ordered a car for them and one of them, or perhaps both of them, asked for a taxi to take them to that new apartment building by the park, Astley House. Your mates must do well, them flats are big money for this town."

They thanked the barman again, sat, drank their wine and picked at a ploughman's lunch between them; adrenalin had taken the place of appetite.

"Now we have four, maybe five targets, dorogoy. We know where they live, is good start, family will be pleased, let's go to this Astley House and look for possibilities."

The apartment building was a boomerang shape with dramatically sloping rooves. The flats in the four-storey development had balconies overlooking the park. The car park had a covered way to secure twin front doors, covered by cameras and an intercom system. There was, Gary, noticed, goods and, he supposed, furniture entrance at the back of the building along a 'Private-no-entry' driveway.

"What you think, Gary?" asked Daria, studying the building, "You see anything useful?"

"Depends on where their flats are, doesn't it? I mean, if they are on the top floor maybe we could doctor the lift, but other than that I have to come to the same conclusion we did with the other homes, they are no good for our purposes, we must think of something else, but knowing where they live has to be a great start."

"It is so, I tell Alex, we are nearly ready. I tell him we have to kill like shoot or hit on head and hide bodies, no other way. We go back to hotel now, yes?"

"Oh yes," said Gary, his lunchtime red wine beginning to work on his loins and his vestiges of morality.

14

Max spotted the flashing red light on his surveillance system as soon as he walked in through his front door. Usually, he'd have an alarm on his phone, but with so much hacking about, he'd limited his vulnerability by closing open-source apps and links. He popped the camera unit's SD card into his laptop and saw the motion detector selected video of a small Ford in his car park area and two people, very suspicious people, he thought, studying his flat and surroundings. Gary knew immediately and instinctively what he was seeing. He called Dan.

"Hey guy," he said, "you and Jo gotta go right now, we've got company already." Oh heck, he thought to himself, I sound like a B-movie.

"What's happened?" asked Dan. Max explained.

"OK, Max, thanks. You know mate, I'm still not happy about leaving you in the lurch, exposed to these bastard maniacs."

"I know, Dan, I know, but it's the only way that makes any sense and, my friend, it's the only way you, we, can protect Jo. Just go, disappear and leave it to me, I owe you that much."

"You don't owe me anything, old chap. You've more than made up for your, er, misjudgement, but I agree about Jo; you and I have been through too much for her to leave her to some barbaric assassin now. We'll go, not telling you where for obvious reasons but I'll let you know what's what when I can, and for God's sake, take care of yourself, Max, you still don't know if and when the cavalry will arrive."

"Yeah, well, Art says his client Jimmy has bitten and he's going to, and I quote, ram a whole new arsehole into those motherfuckers. But you're right, I don't know where the support is coming from, or when but I can take care of myself, don't worry. And Dan…?"

"Yes, Max, what is it?"

"I might do things which you think are a bit off, strange, even going back to my old ways, but I won't be, promise you; what you see, what you hear, it will be for the good long term, please don't doubt me."

"What are you planning Max, you ought to tell me."

"I can't, Dan, just trust me, please. Give my love to Jo. Bye, mate, look after her and yourself too, I care, you know."

Max's first action as a lone warrior was sending stills of the small Ford and close-ups of its occupants to Art. He messaged: 'Hey Art, the baddies are here. It won't be long now. Is help on its way?'

In New York, at his desk on West 40th street, looking out at the New York Times building, Art revelled in his status and luxury and pondered the price he'd had to pay for it. He messaged back: 'Jimmy says he's got it covered. Urgency understood, Photos with him now. Good luck.'

Making Max's strategy a reality wasn't the easy ride Art had hoped for. Even though he knew where Jimmy was living, getting to see him presented problems in the form of layers of security, from bulky bodyguards to tripwires and auto-fired machine gun positions in his grounds. An invitation was essential to survival. Jimmy had responded to Art's request for a meeting. Art had explained that he had information that had to be delivered face-to-face. He'd been told to pick up the company jet for a trip to Costa Rica, where a company car would drive him to Jimmy's isolated villa.

Once the epitome of Latin good looks and devil-may-care-free spirit, Jimmy had matured, aged by stress and the rigours of being a boss in exile. Mistrust and suspicion haunted his dark eyes. His power and cold ruthlessness were as strong as ever and Art felt intimidated in his company even though Jimmy was suave and hospitable and gracious in his welcome.

Art had presented his carefully prepared pitch; all the

motivators and key trigger points had been carefully woven into the narrative. In a humid twenty-seven degrees, Art felt a chill when Jimmy responded to his story.

"You know Art, I've been around the block a few times and I know you are a smart lawyer; your firm costs us enough, you should be smart. But you are playing me Art, you are trying it on with me and that's not wise, my friend, not wise at all."

Art attempted a defence, but Jimmy was in the chair. "OK, I believe some of your tale, I am concerned, really I am, that the guys in the UK are in danger of being hit. OK, leave that to me, and I'll fix it. What I don't believe is this cock and bullshit baloney about a top man staying on or the reasons for wanting us to have the shares on the cheap. Don't make no sense, if they want to run, they'll sell the shares for the highest price, won't they?"

"No sir, their thinking is based on panic; they think they need to get out as fast as possible and to sell you the shares at a family price to ensure a quick, clean get-away."

"Ok, ok, and this guy Max? I remember him, and all about him. Didn't he get all righteous and sanctimonious? Wanted to make up for his namby-pamby crime? Yeah? How come he's turning rogue again? Don't trust it Art, I don't trust it at all."

"Well, sir, my advice, the advice you pay for so you might consider it, is to save Onetelcall and its keeper people if you can and then use Max as you want until you don't need him. It's a hard, cynical world and Max knows the risks. If he isn't being straight, you'll know before he can be any nuisance or danger, I'll know too, I'll keep a close eye on him."

"*If I can, if I can*, you goddam half-arsed little lawyer, *if I can?* I can do fuckin' anything, and you'd better believe it. Onetelcall and its people will be saved, I can do that, I can do what I want, and if I want the company to be a useful family asset, then that is what will happen. You got me Art? Lo entendes?"

Art understood and was mightily relieved.

Jimmy had learned from childhood that you only told lawyers what you wanted them to know and no more; they are no more trustworthy than the feds, he had been told. He didn't share any of his plans with Art, but the moment Art had spun his tale, Jimmy knew exactly what he'd do.

As soon as he went into isolation, Jimmy knew he'd be watched. As he slowly re-established himself as the undisputed family head, he trapped his watchers and pointed out the error of their ways. His watchers were the best in their field, and they knew it. They could find anyone, kill anyone, anywhere, any time. They were never caught. But Jimmy had snared them, luring them with a voluptuous waitress and some doped birria, he recruited them as his personal attack force.

Jesus and Angelo had been family stalwarts and under Jimmy's control, they remained loyal to the whole cohort. They knew the secrets, they knew where the bodies were buried, they'd buried most of them. They knew all about Jimmy, his beautiful cousin Margarita, her banished boyfriend, Onetelcall founder, Ray-Spray Wilson, and their secret hideaway on Jimmy's old ranch in Ecuador. Jesus and Angelo were brothers. Born in the slum area of Mexica City, known as Nezo-Chalco-Itza, their father ran errands for a drug gang working for the Sinaloa cartel and was a methamphetamine addict, their mother tried to earn a living as a prostitute but in a slum of eight million people, there was a lot of competition and very little trade. She too smoked and snorted methamphetamine and died from a massive brain bleed when the boys were four years old.

The brothers had an almost telepathic symbiosis. They had relied on each other from the day their mother died. Their father ignored them, and they never felt love nor understood normal human feelings and emotions. Survival was paramount; it was only survival against all others that mattered. By the time they were ten years old, they were used to seeing death and killings. They only knew base inhumanity and drug-crazed violence; they understood drug wars, how small gangs would kill for a tiny plot of territory or favour from a cartel soldier. They knew nothing else.

Jesus and Angelo shared an innate intelligence, genetic perhaps, maybe one of their parents could have been successful given any chance at all; the boys not only survived but taught themselves how to prosper in their dystopian environment of slum city. Insensate, callous and brutal, Jesus and Angelo had no compunction about killing. People lived, people died, what did it matter? They would live, they would die, and they didn't care. Their impassive and unfeeling nature was spotted by a cartel organiser who gave them a job, jointly, to monitor the activities of allies and competitors, to follow, watch, track and identify anyone or any activity which would be against the cartel's best interests. If necessary, their job included making sure any problem went away, initially with their boss's sanction, and latterly by their own judgement.

When they reached twenty years old, way beyond a slum life expectancy for junior hoodlums, Jesus and Angelo had acquired a reputation for stealth, for finding people in hiding, for tracking those who were escaping their form of correction and for delivering swift, neat, indetectable executions regularly and reliably. Many young men were willing to kill for a pittance, but few had the brothers' guile or cunning; few were of any value to the cartel. Jesus and Angelo proved their worth time and time again and the cartel rewarded them accordingly. They were useful and trustworthy and that made them special.

Jimmy's great uncle, then head of the family, saw their potential as a specialist tracing and killing hit team and took them under his wing. They respected someone for the first time in their lives and shared a rare feeling of gratitude and protectiveness. For as long as they were alive, their new mentor would be safe; his enemies would be their enemies and would die.

Being caught out by Jimmy was a shock. They had been taken in by a pretty face and, off-guard, had eaten food that knocked them out. They were angry with themselves but reflected that the experience would only make them stronger and more invulnerable. They knew Jimmy had gone into hiding after some major catastrophe in Europe but didn't understand the details. When they learned that it was Jimmy who had been behind their abduction, they were surprisingly sanguine. Jimmy's great uncle had been the only human being for whom they felt anything; therefore, Jimmy, by default, must be a good man too and they were willing to accede to his instruction.

Jesus and Angelo had acquired a lot of money over the years. They could easily afford the tools of their trade, private jets, supercars, technology, arms, luxurious living and a film-star lifestyle. When they were commissioned, they charged a large fee, but mainly they worked because they lived for their work. They knew they were top of their tree and enjoyed the challenge and the status. Jimmy saw them differently and treated them as a hunter treats his dogs. They were not house-guests, they were not dinner-guests, they were mercenaries and should be treated as such. He didn't want discussion, he just wanted them to do the job as decreed, so he briefed them by document and printed photographs, nothing digital, and dispatched them to do their work. Where there were questions, the brothers would improvise and make decisions, he knew that. They would succeed because they were the best and they always came through.

Jesus and Angelo flew to a private strip near Los Angeles in their own Hawker 1000 jet, then on to New York as Esteban and Emilio Garcia and on to Schiphol as Miguel and Jose Gonzales. They travelled back to Bristol airport as Riccardo and Mattia Bianchi on Italian passports; the brothers had papers for names and nationalities to suit any journey, any masquerade. They hired a modern evocation of an Austin Healy 3000 from a specialist car hire company, not particularly unobtrusive but it was a car they had wanted since they saw a photograph of one in an old car magazine when they were boys. Roof down, shades on, the sonorous straight six engine booming its power, Jesus and Angelo, endeavouring to drive on the right side of the road, headed off for Olderbury, photographs of Daria and Gary in their project folder.

15

Duggie Miller had been a courier and dogsbody for Olderbury's now jailed drugs organiser, Sniff Taylor. When Max and Dan created an online social media campaign to besmirch Sniff Taylor's character and engineer his subsequent arrest, Max saved Duggie from implication in any crime and then offered him a job in Onetelcall. In his youth, Duggie was insignificance personified, teased that he had to stand up twice to throw a shadow. His brush with social media had left him scarred by online cruelty. Sniff had used him by affecting friendship as a technique for making Duggie do the dodgy jobs Sniff and his 'blokes' didn't want to do. Now, understandably, Duggie was deeply grateful to Max and, with a steady job and secure income, he had managed to build a life far beyond his dreams. He had escaped the squat which had been his home and hiding place and rented a small, but to him, palatial, flat above a newsagent's shop and had made some friends, which was a revelatory experience after his habitual solitude.

When Max invited Duggie for an early evening pint, he was delighted to accept. It was the evening of Dan and Jo's vanishing from Olderbury, and Max needed an ally he could trust.

"Cheers, Duggie," said Max, chinking his wine glass against Duggie's pint mug, "thanks for meeting me."

They were in the lounge bar of The Coopers Arms, a smalltown pub opposite the flat where Jo had been attacked by Duggie's former exploiter, Sniff. It was a quiet pub where the two men could talk safely.

"Duggie, I'm not going to mess about, I need your help. You up for a bit of extramural effort?"

Duggie smiled at his saviour and, he knew, real friend, "Course I am Max, all you've got to do is tell me what you want me to do."

"I'm in danger, Duggie. There's no way of dressing it up. I believe I've got two Eastern European thugs on my case who want revenge for some discoveries about their boss's outrageous social media interference and big-time hacking operations. Duggie, this isn't a leg-pull and I'm not being dramatic, and I want you to know that there may be some danger for you if you agree to help, and, by the way, there's no reason why you should, you owe me nothing now, so if you'd rather keep to a quiet life I would understand totally."

"Like I said, Max, just tell me what you want me to do. I'll have your back; you know I will."

"That's exactly it Duggie, I'd appreciate it if you could tail me for the next few days. I'm certain someone will have a pop at me and I want to take any precautions I can. One of the best ways I can see is to ask you to follow me at a distance and get on your mobile to me the moment you spot anyone else following me or acting strange close to me. You ok with that? I'll make it worth your while and do all I can to keep you safe, of course."

"Look, Max," said Duggie appearing a little offended, "I'm thrilled to be able to help you. Like it or not, I do owe you but that's not the main reason, it's for me too. You see, I don't often get a chance to do something out of the ordinary or in the slightest way brave. I'm not a brave man you know, and sometimes I pray for an opportunity to prove myself to me, just once, so don't talk to me, please, about making it worth my while, you're doing me a service, you are, just by asking me and, of course, I'll do it. I won't let you down Max and, as it goes, I'm pretty good at following people unseen in the shadows. Sniff made me follow people who owed him money quite often, so yes, Max, I'm your man and it's bloody marvellous that you've asked me, that you think I am up to the job and that you trust me, thank you man, thank you."

Max was moved. He had always thought that there was, or could be, more to Duggie than first impressions might suggest.

"Ok, mate, it's a deal, but you must know how grateful I am

to you. I don't know whether I'm putting you in front of a gun or not and yet you don't ask, you don't hesitate, you're some chum Duggie, somebody to reckon with, I'd say."

Duggie's world was complete.

"Tell you what, Max, you just act as normal, if anyone is watching you, you don't want to alarm them or do anything which says you're on to them. Yeah?"

Max agreed.

"So, the best plan is for me to tail you from a distance all the time and to do that I'll have to follow you home, park up in the dark and stay in the car until you go out again, and then I'll keep behind you, but you won't see me, and nobody should be able to spot me in the distance, away from you. That the sort of thing you want, what you had in mind?"

"That's absolutely what I had in mind, Duggie and, when this is all over, which it will be, I'm going to buy you the biggest, best dinner you've ever had. And bring that nice Kathy I've seen you hob-nobbing with at work if you like."

Duggie's world was even more complete.

"So, Duggie, you ought to know who you are looking out for. Here," Max handed two print-out photos to Duggie, "these two characters are the ones I think are after me. Pretty easy to spot, eh? She's a looker and he'd stand out in a crowd too. I hope it makes your job a bit easier. I don't know, but I don't think anyone else is involved."

"Thanks, Max, no problem. I'll see them if they come anywhere near you."

"You sure you're ok with all this? I mean, it means sleeping, or even better not sleeping, in your car, is that OK with you?"

"Yeah, it's ok. I've done it before, I'll be fine, don't worry."

Max noticed that Duggie suddenly looked a little ashamed; he couldn't know that Duggie was remembering the time he'd spent in his car outside Jo's flat as ordered by Sniff Taylor when he was planning his assault on her.

"OK then, Duggie, let's do it. I'm going back to the office now and then I'll be going home. OK?"

"Wagons roll!" Duggie grinned happily as he trotted off to his car. "Actually, Max," he called as they were leaving, "ok if I nip home first to get some stuff, I'll catch you at the office in, say, half an hour?"

"Course it is Duggie, course it is."

The next stage in Max's plan was to risk using email, much against Dan's wishes and the Alliance's methodologies, but he had to give the full story to the people he knew and could trust in the Alliance.

Back in the office, Max opened the file containing the report he and Jo had prepared for Dan and set to the task of expanding with all the latest occurrences. He had decided to tell the Alliance about Dan and Jo's run for safety and to include details of who he believed to be his would-be assailants. He had decided against giving the Alliance any information about the American-Mexican interests and plans for Onetelcall. He certainly wasn't going to say that he'd enlisted the support of who he knew to be criminals on a grand scale, not that he had proffered a spurious promise, hopefully, of helping then make Onetelcall a foreign power trolling subsidiary.

Max looked at his watch. The evening was rushing by, ten o'clock already, which meant five o'clock in Ohio. He called Harvey Schuster, Dan's appointed replacement CEO.

"Hey Harv, how they hangin'?" chuckled Max into a new mobile phone and cash sim he'd bought in a supermarket.

"That you Max, gotta new number?"

"Precautions, just precautions. How's it been going?"

"Oh man, you won't believe it, Christ, I mean, it's a fucking war in cyberspace. There are bad guys everywhere you look.

Since we set up our team here for the Alliance, we just keep finding more and more real dirt, and I mean stuff that gets governments thrown out, encourages civil war, motivates madmen, I mean man, it's fucking crazy. I tell you, man, what we're doing here in Ohio for Dan's Alliance is awesome stuff. We've identified loads of bandits all over cyberspace, malware, ransomware, denial of service, identity and password theft, email hijacking, cyber-heists, crypto-crime, the whole fucking gamut man, a big nine yards of keyboard marauders. It's manic, man, just manic. Tell you what, though, Max, and I suppose it isn't in our remit from Dan but cracking some of the encrypted networks those fucking terrorists use out of places like Pakistan and Iran is just about impossible. People say they are just tribal warmongers, but I tell you this, there are some mighty smart dudes behind their cyber-stuff. But if we aren't close to terrorist stuff yet, others are, I know, so we've focused on the day-to-day cybercrime and social engineering as they call it."

Max was about to interrupt, but Harvey was warming to his subject.

"While you guys are chasing goddam reds, we are onto the big stuff, oh man, it's big stuff, alright. China, man, they're something else. Like half a billion posts and messages, a year come outta that place. They got armies of guys called Wumao, apparently, that means 50 cent-ers, 'cos that's what they get for each social media post they spew out. They call 'em Cyberspace Administration Bureaus and organise themselves into squadrons, brigades and detachments, those are trollers who work remotely from the farms, like in universities and so on. They are all youngsters, totally indoctrinated and they'll do and say anything the party tells them.

"Tell ya, Max, it's an eye-opener, that's for sure and, guess what? They're not too difficult to spot when you've got your troll-finder glasses on. They all have usernames like tell-the-truth6756xx, and howitisharry000777, and so on, quite pathetic if it wasn't so goddam evil. They all use similar language and often hit platforms simultaneously with the same messages. None of them has any followers, of course. But oh boy, do they create havoc. When you've got time, I'll tell you how much they've cost big firms like Nike and Adidas, like Toyota and Disney, man, it's unbelievable.

"We've got hard evidence of how they stirred up all the anti-vaxxers, like puppets having their strings pulled, how they managed social media suppression of news they didn't want bandied about on the platforms, man, it's… and don't get me started on the others, the Russians and… and, oh God…"

"Look, Harv, I know all too well that it's a helluva thing, but we've got, er as you Americans say, a situation here in Olderbury and I wanted to tell you about it myself before you hear rumours, you know what misinformation can do."

Harvey chuckled.

By the end of the call, Max had told Harvey everything including, with a strictly not for the Alliances' ears agreement, most of the details about the share sale offer to the shareholders and his hopes that they may help protect him from any reprisals. Again, he kept any mention of Onetelcall being groomed for trolling to himself.

"Shit man, shit, you know shit spreads, eh? We in danger here, do you reckon? I guess we've kinda known we were tweaking a tiger by its tail when we started this stuff for Dan and his collection of cyber guys, and actually, I've put some measures in place here just in case."

"You have?" Max was intrigued.

"Yeah man, for sure, like I hate our gun laws but I gotta tell you, I'm carryin' these days, so's most of my forensic team, as I say, just in case."

"That's probably very wise," said Max, wondering if it was at all wise.

"Hey guy, you want that I come over or send some boys to ride shotgun with you?"

"That's a kind thought, you bloody cowboy, but I'll be ok and, anyway, it might be too late already."

"Oh fuck, Max. Keep your sad arse away from bullets, eh?"

"Thanks, Harv, you're a pal. See you on the other side, if there is one."

Neither of them quite knew what that meant.

Max thumbed the new phone's red button and thought about Duggie. He called and Duggie took some time to answer.

"It's Max."

Duggie sounded disbelieving, "Oh yeah? That you Max? It's not your phone."

"It's me, Duggie, not an imposter, honest. Look, I've got this throw-away phone and it occurred to me that you should have one too, just in case we are being listened too. How about you pop into the 24-hour supermarket and buy one too, with an instant SIM? I'll be here for another thirty or forty minutes anyway, so we'll pick up again when you get back; just be sure to call me as soon as you've fired up your new phone. OK?"

"Ok, Kemosabe, I'm on my way."

"Why does everyone want to be a cowboy tonight?" said Max, quietly to himself.

He spent another twenty minutes 'putting his affairs in order', as his father used to say when he reviewed his will with his son. After another twenty minutes on letters and instructions for his friends, colleagues and employees, he was ready to leave. He didn't have to wait long before his new phone squirmed about on the desk as it vibrated with an incoming call.

"Well, it works then," said Duggie, "I'm on my new phone. You got the number now?"

"Great, Duggie, I've got you. Let's leave now, shall we? I'm going home but I want to take a detour. If you lose me, I'll be going via the Royal George's car park and then on to my flat,

OK?"

"Got you, Max."

Wishing he'd thought of hiring a car for another layer of cloaking, Max fired up his racy Audi and made for the hotel. In his mirror, he could catch an occasional glimpse of Duggie's Ford Focus way back behind him. It took Max just a few seconds to see the car he'd spotted on his security tape. He called Duggie, who had parked on the roadside some fifty metres away.

"Looks like the dynamic duo is tucked up in bye-byes for the night. It's nearly midnight; I wouldn't think they'd be up to anything now. Home time for us, you sure you're ok with this and being in your car all night?"

"Max, it might be unlikely that those vermin will come out tonight, but you don't know for sure. They wouldn't be too good at their jobs if they were predictable, would they? I'll be where they can't see me and, as far as I can help it, you'll be as safe as poss."

Max drove home and parked in his usual spot. Duggie followed him at some distance; no one would have noticed he was a tail.

And nobody noticed a classic English sports car burbling through the town and out towards Max's flat, following at a professional, experienced, discrete distance from Duggie.

16

"Alex? Daria."

"No shit, who else?"

"Mudak," responded Daria. "That's shithead to you, Gary," she added to Gary, who was listening in by her side. "Alex, we need talk now."

"It's gone midnight, why do you have to call at this hour, what's wrong with morning?"

"You're the guy telling us to hurry, Alex, so listen to me, then you get all the beauty sleep you need."

"That'll be a lot then," added Gary, slightly drunk.

"Oh please, you two, grow up. We have big job, and one wants to sleep and other make jokes. This is not family way. Right Daria, you are right; please say what you have to say," responded Alex.

"I make report and recommendations, OK?"

"Like a sit-rep, or is that shit-rep?"

"Shut up Gary."

"He been drinking? Not good, should be not drinking, need clear head for this work."

"He'll be OK Alex, now, let's get back to business," replied Daria, digging Gary hard in the ribs with her elbow, no pleasure-pain this time. "I have told you we know who we have target. There are, we say, five persons, they are Dan Rackham and Jo, his wife, Max Golby and two females who seem to be the ones who did spying, they are Sue Cox and Indira Bhatt."

"Get on with it Daria, I know all that already."

Daria remained calmly systematic.

"We see where they live and we decide no opportunities for accident at any home. You agreed this, remember?"

Alex was losing his temper rapidly.

"Daria, don't mess with me, get to the point now."

"We have choice, Gary says, we either shoot or we kidnap. Then we take bodies and hide somewhere, bury perhaps if we can."

"Yes, Daria, I understand all that. What's the problem? Why do you have to you call me this time of night, to tell me what I know eh?"

"I, we, Gary, we need support. We need good gun. I have my pistol but perhaps it is not good for distance shot. Gary says he shoot good with rifle. We have one, please?"

"Yep."

"We need bigger car, I think. Small car we got, no room for one body, not room for more than one body either. You supply from somewhere else and deliver to me, we not rent car locally now, too easy to trace."

"Yep."

"We need strong man…"

"Whaddya mean, I'm strong enough, we don't need bought-in muscle," Gary objected.

"We need strong man to help bury and to be in fight if it happens. Gary, dorogoy, you strong too of course, but not fighter, not big digger, and you need energy for me."

Gary grinned lasciviously.

"Yep."

"That's it, Alex, all good?"

"Yeah, all good, I'll arrange for a good gun, a rifle now, tonight and get Brian to bring to you in the van tomorrow, what is later today now, I think. Then I report to the family at home;

they ask lots of times what's happening, I need to tell now."

"Who's Brian," asked Gary, wary suddenly despite the effects of the wine he'd consumed.

"Not worry Gary," replied Alex, "Brian works on the farm. He is very big, very strong, not very clever. You say 'dig', he digs, you say 'fight', he fights. You explain why but he doesn't understand, he is right for you."

"Good, thank you," said Daria, "we need to be ready in morning, I think. We not have time to follow these people to see where they go when, so we have to take our luck. We start with Dan Rackham soon as Brian gets to us."

Brian, tall, thick-set and muscular from farm work, got to The Royal George by breakfast time.

"Alright?" said Brian by way of greeting, recognising his two contacts from the photographs Alex had shown him.

Daria and Gary nodded in return.

"I'm fuckin starving. You two going to stand me a bustin' hotel brekky then?"

"We have very short time, no time for sitting hotel eating fat fried food," declared Daria sniffily, already not liking Brian one little bit.

"Oh yeah? Well, I'll tell ya lady. I missed me dinner last might, I've been driving for half the fuckin night, I'm knackered and fuckin hungry. You want me to do anything else today, I want breakfast, capisce?"

Daria and Gary sipped bitter, hotel urn breakfast coffee as Brian had what the menu described as King George's Royal Full House Breakfast. He anointed his two fried eggs with large dollops of red sauce, making his plate, thought Daria, more like a Royal shooting accident than a meal. Brian ate noisily, wielding his utensils like dumpers and diggers. Trying to ignore the slurpy sounds of open-mouthed mastication, Daria outlined her plan.

"I think we go to doors and persuade to come with us, better and safer than trying to kidnap in street. Now we have Brian, we can persuade most effectively and then we put them in van go where Gary can deal with them."

Gary wasn't sure whether to be further offended by Daria's undisguised confidence in Brian's masculinity or to panic about how he was going to do the 'dealing with'.

Brian eventually leant back, wiping the remnants of sauce and grease from the corners of his mouth, "Bloody marvellous," he announced, "right then, you two miserable fuckers, let's go outside to play."

Gary went to get their hire car and Daria walked with Brian to his van.

"Brian,"

"Steady on girl sounded almost matey for a moment."

"Brian, listen, not speak. You follow us, Gary drive that car there," she pointed at their hire car, "not follow close, you understand, not be obvious."

"OK love, whatever you say. But here's a thought, what if I lose you and, for another thing, what happens when we get to wherever we are going?"

"Don't try think, Brian, we think, we keep in touch on phone, you have us on one-key dial, we have you. When we get to destination, I call you, tell you where you put van. Understand this, Brian?"

"Got ya, darlin. Boss gave me this brand-new phone specially for your little shindig; make sure you've got the right number, won't you?"

Daria ignored his mocking, familiar tone.

"British mudak," she muttered as she got into the car. "Alex's man, that Brian, better be strong and ready for job, so far he is idiot."

Gary smiled happily; somehow, he always construed Daria's criticism of another man as an implied accolade for him. His head was still a little fuzzy from the previous night's excesses and he drove slowly away from the hotel towards Dan and Jo's village home.

At the entrance to the village, Gary pulled into a gateway and got out to check if it was likely to be in use. The old five-bar gate, hanging haphazardly from rusted hinges, hadn't been opened for years. Gary nodded to Daria, who phoned her instructions to Brian, who accordingly parked his van in the gateway and followed the car on foot.

Outside Dan and Jo's house, the three unlikely visitors stood in the driveway.

"Looks like no-one's at home, dunnit, bit of a cock-up on the planning front, is it?" Brian remarked chippily.

"Ring doorbell Gary."

Gary rang three times before concluding that Brian was right.

"They run away, I think," said Daria tersely, "wish we could see inside."

"No prob darlin'," said Brian brightly. "Me, I'm a bit of a housebreaker on the quiet. Well, you got to be quiet about it ain't ya, anyway, I can get you in there if you want."

"Stupid, house will have alarm all over it, is owned by security specialist, it is not for common burglar."

"Fuck off, darlin," replied Brian evenly, "I'll bet you a quickie I can get in there without setting off any alarms; in fact, not only that, I'll kill all the alarms too and let you two in by the front door, how's that for an offer?"

"Good offer indeed, Brian," replied Daria, smiling for the first time that morning.

"Hang on," said Gary, in what sounded like a squawk, "he's making a bet with you, Daria and if he gets us in, you give him a quickie. Do you know what that means?"

"Yes, Gary, with you, I learn full meaning of quickie."

Brian laughed gustily; Gary turned red and very angry.

"Brian," Daria saw the need to quell Gary's rising ire, "no quickie for you today but now you say you can break in, you keep your balls if you succeed, you lose them if you fail, how's that for an offer?"

"Ok, ok, you keep your little pet here happy; I'll do it for you anyway, I like a bit of fun."

Gary's natural vindictiveness made Brian a marked man in his books; one way or another, he'd pay the chump for that 'pet' jibe.

"Gimme a minute, just need a couple of bits from the van and I'll be back."

Big man though Brian was, his ability to climb a stone wall using only his sturdy long-blade knife and some home-fashioned pitons impressed his two onlookers. Within ten minutes, he was balancing on a slightly proud stone in the wall, his knife addressing the latch of a rear bedroom window.

"Even clever fuckers don't worry so much about upstairs windows they think can't be reached," Brian whisper-shouted down to his comrades.

His knife made short work of the jamb liner to expose the rails and, quickly, the sash cords. As he expected, he found some alarm wires hidden in the frame and, with experienced knife-work again, spliced and re-joined the wires. A quick flick of the sash lock with his blade and Brain completed his silent entry.

As he opened the front door, Brian said, "Told ya, who's stupid now then eh? I'll be claiming my prize one day, love." He winked at Gary, who visibly seethed in response. Brian laughed again.

"This clever man, he not leave evidence here I think, but we look carefully anyway, might find something we can use."

Brian opted out of the search stating, correctly in Daria's view, that he wouldn't recognise something useful if he trod on it. After an hour of thumbing through book pages, nosing through drawers and generally poking about, neither Daria nor Gary had found anything worthwhile.

"Might as well call it a day," said Gary, "nothing here, they've taken everything useful, just left an old laptop in that backroom there."

Daria's instincts were piqued. She rushed to the room Gary had indicated and found the old laptop quickly. More in hope, she pressed the 'on' button and the screen lit up. She heard the old hard drive whir and click, and a fatal error message appeared; the laptop then shut itself down.

"Is no good, this machine. We leave it, it can tell us nothing," declared Daria. "Actually, there is nothing here for us anyway; we leave, I think."

Brian carefully eradicated any trace of their entry and search before walking back to his van. He opened the sliding side door and put his climbing aids back in their box. Out of habit, he checked that the rifle Alex had asked him to take was still safely in its hiding place, along with a stock of ammunition. He took the weapon out, stroked it fondly and took aim through the red dot sight at a passing pigeon which he lit up and tracked across the sky before carefully putting the gun back in its case. He felt a tremor of excitement as he drove the van out of the layby, steering around a sporty English sports car that had been parked in front of him.

Daria, too, was in a state of heightened excitement. The thought of being in on a kill had stimulated all of her basic feral, carnal senses. The mental imagery of muscular, strong Brian claiming his quickie prize had excited her even more. She looked at Gary as he settled into the passenger seat and felt an impulsive, compulsive need to torment him. She reached across and dug her fingernails into his upper thigh; even through his jeans, she knew her claw-like grip would hurt.

"What's that for?"

"You jealous, you think of me and Brian having quickie and you hate, you want Daria, nobody else can have, that's right, isn't it?"

It was true, Gary had been consumed by anger and jealousy at the thought of brutish Brian and Daria being together.

"Me? Jealous? Of that lout? Oh yeah, not."

As Daria dug in more deeply, Gary's breath got shorter. Her left hand slid further up Gary's thigh and reached his now prominent bulge. While her left hand grabbed Gary's ardour, her right hand suggestively fondled her own left breast. Gripping hard again, she drove Gary to the edge.

"Now you think of me, eh Gary? Now you want Daria," she whispered as she put both hands back on the steering wheel, smiling at Gary's obvious predicament.

"You sit on hands, Gary, no cheating, no relief for you in car. Nothing for you until work is done. Now we go for the man Max. Now you plan your kill."

Two well-dressed men wearing sunglasses walked past the car as Daria sped off.

17

"Hey, Max."

"Hi, Harv."

"Max, it's blowing up man, the systems are alive with intel and I gotta tell ya, you gotta take care man, I do believe you could be hit and soon."

"What's happening, Harv?" asked Max more calmly than he felt.

"It's all fucking happening Max. You handy for your laptop?"

"Yeah," said Max opening his machine.

"I sent you an email, it's a snap of a lady who is, we think, your would-be assassin; if it isn't her, she's sure part of the party that's out to get you."

Max opened the email and saw an upwards-angled screenshot of a pretty woman staring at the screen cam that captured her image.

"Got her Max? Your cunning old boss rigged a duff laptop in his home just for this eventuality. Anyone breaking into his pad and sneaking a peek at the laptop he left behind gets nabbed; the picture was automatically flashed through to our Alliance comms unit. We know who she is, of course."

"And…"

"And one of our trojan mares has scored with a Moldovan stallion!" Harvey Schuster was bursting with elation. "We got a load of messages from some guy called Alex to a location we know as a state-sponsored troll farm in Moldova, the messages say this broad and two guys are tasked with targeting you, Dan, Jo and your two girls, Indira and Sue. Max, this is for real and I'm like truly worried for you. You got precautions? Got any protection? Any back-up, man?"

"Does this mean, of course, it does, that this woman has already been to Dan's place this morning? I mean, when was this photo taken?"

"No more than ten minutes ago, man, that's why I'm on the horn right now; it's a warning, man, take cover for fucks sake."

"Ok, Harv, thanks. I'll be in touch."

"God, I hope so, man, I hope so."

Max picked up his 'Duggie' phone. "They are on their way Duggie. Don't know about you, but I'm in no mood to fight if we can hide and see what happens; what do you say?"

Duggie didn't need convincing. He'd spent much of the night planning how to avoid being shot at in defence of his friend.

"Max, I've had a thought. We know they are coming for you but let's not make it easy, eh? Let's make 'em work for it. Why don't we hide like right now, somewhere we can see what's going on and who's doing it?"

"OK, Duggie, I'm getting out of my flat now, meet you in the stables across the yard from my car?"

"You bet."

Duggie had already parked his car in a partially hidden spot at the back of the old farm buildings. He left it, hitting the central locking button as he ran towards the stables. He found Max in the stable building and, one by one, they scurried up a loft ladder to the roof void. Hidden behind a broken hayloft door, they could see out over the farmyard to Max's front door.

"This is exciting, isn't it?" said Duggie, feeling more alive than he'd ever felt before.

"No, it bloody isn't mate, it's fucking terrifying."

"I've got a surprise present for you, Max," said Duggie surreptitiously.

Max looked at Duggie, who was proffering a small Berretta 9000 pistol.

"It was one of Sniff's. I, er, borrowed it before he was nicked."

"Loaded?"

"Oh yeah, loads itself, see. Nine mil, it's a killer mate, a real good gun. Sniff got it off some Scotch yob who was on the lamb. Got a pocketful of ammo too, but that's all. Here."

Max took the compact, surprisingly heavy little pistol; it felt reassuring.

"You or me?"

"Me, Max, I'll have it. You're the target, I'm the back-up. You could get shot trying to aim; I can hit 'em without warning. Me, Max."

Max nodded his agreement. "You're full of surprises, Duggie; good man, thank you."

Astonished at his assertiveness, Duggie felt a rare sense of self-pride.

"We're making up for it, aren't we, Max?"

Max's car, still in its usual parking space, was soon joined by another. The girl Max had just seen in Harvey's picture got out of the driver's door and a man, possibly mid-thirties, clambered out of the passenger's door. He was limping slightly and moved awkwardly. Two minutes later, Max and Duggie heard another engine in the rural peace. They couldn't see another vehicle but a few seconds after the engine noise died, a tall, strong-looking man carrying what looked like a slim shotgun appeared by the girl's side.

"Fuck," muttered Max, feeling the cold reality of evident danger.

The woman walked to Max's front door and, Max could see, pushed the doorbell button. Then she knocked on the door with fist knuckles.

"Car is here, search everywhere," Max heard the woman command.

Max and Duggie moved back to take deeper refuge behind some straw bales. Still able to glimpse out, Max could see the big man looking at the walls and windows of his apartment.

"Fuck, he's only fucking casing my flat; I think he's going to break in, the bastard," whispered Max.

Duggie nodded, his mouth clamped shut.

"Oi darlin, you want to have a guided tour of this luxurious countryside apartment?"

"Not bother here, quickie-man, no point."

Daria intuitively knew that Max was close by, she also knew they would probably not find him, certainly not trap him or capture him as planned. She made a decision.

"You hear me Max Golby? We want talk to you. You hide from us now, but we will see you again very soon. We stay in town, in hotel. You come to talk; you know why. You safe for now. You not come to talk, you no longer safe. You hear me? I know you do."

Gary was astonished.

"Why did you do that?"

"What else I do? He see us for sure; he know we are here and that we come for him. What else can I do?"

Gary looked unsure but said no more.

The sound of another car, a powerful car, boomed through the peace as it passed the farm entrance. The car stopped and Daria decided it was time to leave.

"Hey, big man, we are through here, no one at home, we come back for sure. Let's go now; we have more calls to make."

Max and Duggie heard two doors slam and the car started up

and drove off. Seconds later, another door slammed, and Max caught a glance of a van driving out of the side entrance next to the old milking shed. He and Duggie waited for a minute or two longer, and when all was quiet, they emerged from their hideaway and descended to the empty yard.

"They've been to Dan's, and they've been here. I reckon they'll go for the girls next," said Max, "follow me and fast."

Max heard that powerful motor start and race away as he ran towards his car. He took the back road to the far side of Olderbury, where Astley House apartments rose above the town park's greenery. He parked on a sideroad which had a rear gate into the apartment block's service area. He ran up the stairs and hammered on the door. He waited and hammered again, his eyes firmly fixed on the landing windows through which he could see the road and the entrance lane. Pulling out his usual phone, he called Sue Cox's number.

"Sue, where are you? Where's Indira?"

"Max, hi, yeah, we are together and a long way from Olderbury like Dan told us. You alright? You sound flummoxed. Where are you?"

"Outside your flat waiting for a bunch of baddies who mean to do us harm," replied Max as lightly as he could manage.

"Oh, I see, well, for heaven's sake, take care, go somewhere else, why don't you? Stay safe, please Max."

The familiar car drew to a stop outside the apartment block's main entrance and the same two, man and woman, got out again. Max took a business card from his phone cover pocket and wrote on it:

Go back to the hotel. I will contact you.

After jamming the card into the door frame, he turned to run to the rear stairs; as he did so, he saw the same van again, the same big man again. This time, Max's fear lessened; the slight void created by his reduced dread was replaced by increasing anger. He leapt down the stairs, swinging from the banister rail to jump a stage at a time. He reached the rear service door in seconds and, pausing to peer through the small safety glass window to make sure no one was on their way in that way, pushed his way out and ran for cover behind the foliage of the rear terrace.

Only twenty yards or so to his car and Max began to feel confident. He turned away from the shrubs and saw his reflection in the dark lenses of sunglasses. His confidence turned to quivering, shrinking terror. As the sunglasses moved back, another pair of sunglasses appeared from another bush. Under both pairs, there was a sun-tanned, white-toothed smile, and then both pairs vanished into the verdure. At that moment, Max knew that Dan's ploy for protection from Spray's former drug cohort had been successful. His confidence returned. He reached for his Duggie-phone.

"Hey Tonto, you Ok?"

"Yep, masked man, just fine. Just got back to my car, about fifty yards from yours. I take it you are still in the flower beds?"

"On my way, buddy got lots to tell you that even you didn't see."

"You mean the two guys in sunglasses? Are they your cavalry now then?"

"How the fuck did you see them, Duggie?"

"Getting good at this following lark, ain't I?"

Duggie sniggered at Max's amazement. He was having a good day.

"You're a bloody marvel, Duggie, that's for sure. Look, I'm hungry and thirsty, and I'm not going back to the flat. How about a quick pint and sarnie at The Carps?"

Over a pint of best bitter and a couple of cheese and mustard sandwiches, which might have been made a decade ago, Max and Duggie compared notes and thoughts.

"So, Max, as I see it, you've got an Audi, a Ford, another Ford, a van and a gorgeous Healy all playing follow-the-leader in convoy," chuckled Duggie, surprised that he found something funny in the middle of what would have terrified him to a standstill a few days ago.

"Yeah, there's me, Dan, Jo, Sue and Indira as targets; the dark girl, her gimpy boyfriend and some goon as travelling killers; you as under-cover cover and two walking sunglasses who, we believe, will protect us all from the other lot; that about right?"

"Seems so."

"Then the odds are better than they were, even in our favour with a bit of luck. Now we've got two ambitions. One is to stay alive, the other is to capture those murderous shits who represent everything we've been fighting."

"Staying alive I can live with, catching killers, I'm not so sure about, to be honest. Can I have another pint?"

"Sure, look, Duggie, I've got a bit of a plan, a ruse as you might say."

"Oh God, I don't like the sound of that."

"I've said I'm going to contact them at their hotel, The George, and so I will. I'll meet them in the bar; got to be safe, yeah? You'll be there discretely, of course, and perhaps, our sun-shy friends will be local too."

"Ok, so then what? What will you say?"

"Ah, I haven't got that far yet. Get me a pint too, I need some brain food."

While Duggie was at the bar, Max called Harvey.

"Fuck, am I glad to hear your voice," yelled Harvey as soon as he picked up.

"Yes, safe and sound for now anyway, seems I've got some protection, but I won't go into that now."

"Glad to hear it. What's happening there now?"

"I'm just about to ring the people who want to kill me to arrange to meet them for a drink."

"You're fuckin crazy, man. Are you serious?"

"Yep, I'm going to try to catch them or turn them, not sure which yet."

"Turn them as in double agent type crap, that what you mean? No chance man, that girl, the blonde pretty one, she's family, she's born into it, born cruel, born evil, I tell you, she'll die before split, or more accurately, she'll kill you twice, once for being you and once for trying to make her turn in her family. Get the idea?"

"Yeah, I got that Harv, thanks for the boost. Anything else I should know?"

"Well, we've tracked this guy, Alex. We think he's the girl- her name is Daria by the way, we think he's her co-ordinator, the link between her and the family HQ in Chisinau, that's in Moldova you know. The Alex traffic comes from a farmhouse in North Oxfordshire."

"That so, Daria, you say. Thanks. What about her companion, the chap who's always with her, any intel on him?"

"We think his name is Gary Watkins, a recovering alcoholic. We think he met the lovely Daria when she was planted in a rehab; that's how they sell their gear, by the way."

"Inhuman, cynical shits."

"You're right there, bud. Anyway, from what we can tell from Alex's traffic, they're setting this Gary fella up as a fall guy; he's supposed to do the killing and after that, he'll be expendable. Reading between the lines of Alex's reports, Daria has got this Gary aching and ga-ga for her; he'll do anything she tells him. He believes they'll live happily ever after, but Alex is reckoning on popping him off too, neat, no loose ends."

"Harv, have you got any words you can ping to me that show what the plans for this Gary character really are?"

"I'll look, bud and send you what I can right away."

"I'll buy you the best Baberton chicken next time I'm over. Thanks, pal."

"You're welcome; no more goddam lardy chicken though, please!"

Ten minutes later and the second pint half consumed, Max's phone trilled with an incoming message. Harvey had sent a transcript of interrupted messages between Alex and the Moldovan HQ, quite clearly stating that the plan would be to dispose of Gary once he'd done the deeds as instructed by Daria.

Now Max had a plan.

He tapped out a lengthy note and sent it to Art Pincher.

18

Outside the front door of Sue Cox's flat in Astley House, Daria read the note left by Max and fumed with anger. Her plan no longer had the surprise element; Max had jumped one step ahead and she felt outsmarted. Daria Druta had not battled her way through life so far to be outwitted by some English idiot. She had survived and prospered by being the best at outwitting others in everything.

Daria had been born into a poverty-torn, corrupt, crime-ridden, murderous 1990s Moldova where unemployment was overwhelming, and inflation hit over one hundred per cent. Her mother, Daniella and her father, Florin, were both in their late twenties when she was born. Both had been born into 'Familie Odin', an association of mobsters who styled themselves on the mafia. Familie had members in useful positions in food and wine production, export, government, police, and shipping. They were not short of competitors. In 1990s Moldova, crime was, for many, the only survival option. Moldova had become a favoured location for arranged murders where a hit could be bought for next to nothing. Back then, the Moldovan Leu ran at about four to the dollar; by the 2020s, the exchange rate had improved to around twenty to the dollar. In the 1990s, you could have a queue of eager men willing to kill for less than a thousand dollars.

Familie Odin had ranks of cut-throats, executioners and shooters who they deployed swiftly to control any encroachments on their many and varied enterprises. Such freelancers were rewarded with lethal Vint, an injectable concoction of ephedrine from cold and cough remedies, mixed with aspirin and vinegar or with iodine and red phosphorus scraped from the sides of match boxes. This moonlight drug induced a massive energy rush and, for some, a sexual frenzy. Vint also caused rapid bone decay and vein collapse, but for an all-too-short-term buzz, Familie Odin killers loved it, craved it, would kill for it and die for it.

Daria's earliest memories were of lots of people in her home. Daniella and Florin had a comparatively lavish large house in the Telecentru district. All sorts of people visited and often stayed for rich dinners, late-night parties, and sumptuous bedrooms. Guests were Russians, Iranians, some Americans and Mexicans, mainly men from the CIS countries from Azerbaijan to Ukraine. Away from the swish rooms, Daria also saw heavily made-up women and pale, slack-jawed men hidden away in the basement rooms. She saw them inject their drugs, drink potent Mead, Vishinata and Tuica until they could drink no more. She saw them frantically copulating in drug-crazed bacchanalian delirium. She saw them with guns and knives, and she saw them, heard them, being dispatched to their tasks from seduction to slaughter.

Daniella and Florin ensured that Daria was educated, very well educated. She grew up being tutored in maths, languages, sciences, classics and culture. She saw death and barbarism in everything she learned; in art, in literature, she absorbed evil and ignored compassion. Daria learned that the life of others had no value. She saw the lascivious, salacious and lubricious but could not understand love and empathy. At eighteen, roundly and comprehensively educated, Daria was expected to go to university, perhaps Oxford, where she was expected to excel. Sophisticated and mentally agile, slim, blue-eyed and mesmerising, Daria, it seemed, had grown into the complete woman who could anticipate a glowing, successful future.

As she grew and learned, Daria watched her parents, listened to conversations, overhead telephone calls, occasionally followed people of interest, read documents in the home offices and asked questions of everyone who visited. They were innocent, insignificant questions from which Daria built pictures and maps of her parents' life and occupations. She understood psychology and she knew she was solipsistic and selfish beyond any normality. She was fascinated by the power of sex, violence, torture and all forms of control. She relished the coercive influence of drug supply. She lusted for the thrill of inflicting pain and death. Daria did not readily understand jokes and humour, but to see a man shaking with dread until he lost all bodily control would make her howl with laughter.

She eschewed further education for a career in Familie Odin. The senior members welcomed her with glee, tinged with a little apprehension at managing such an indurate, callous, ambitious young lady. She wanted to know all the businesses from the bottom to the top; she wanted to do an apprenticeship, and she would have no weaknesses and no gaps in her knowledge. For two years, she toured the offices of Familie Odin plants. She learned about food and wine production and export, she learned about drug trans-shipping, she learned about bribery and threat. She learned about honeytraps and extortion, savagery, sadism and delivering death to order. She was fascinated by the endless scope of the web and the potential of social media to carry Familie Odin from its poverty-stricken Soviet roots into the cosmopolitan, liberal twenty-first century. She had no interest in becoming a technologist, she preferred to devise techniques, develop disruptive ideas and methods, and expand the burgeoning yield from Familie Odin's digital prowess.

The Chisinau hub and its sister Centre Two flourished due to Daria's innovative thinking. Its trolling and hacking teams, learning from techniques developed in China and by Pakistan-based terrorist communication cells, the Familie Odin's reputation in the black-hat world was established and revered. Her greatest coup was securing the Familie investment to develop an infrastructure capable of serving state-sponsored covert social engineering and orchestrated foreign social media mayhem with the Centre Two facility. She had exploited her sexuality, sensuality and dominatrix entrapment to the full. She kept images and videos of several senior officers from several governments to assure the longevity of the activity. She was also able to keep the Familie's state clients hooked with a flow of temptations. She illustrated the opportunities that being able to hack pacemakers might offer; being able to spike the heart rhythm of a dissident diplomat or dangerous drug dealer with a few keystrokes had considerable appeal.

Daria was early in identifying the theft and manipulation scope presented by a nerd-driven cryptocurrency framework; the more smug the industry was about its invulnerability, the more accessible it became. After proving that her pet tech team could hack and control most cars and aeroplanes, the seniors of Familie Odin eventually decided it was time for Daria to develop more skills and expand her horizons with some missionary work. The ever-growing market of the United Kingdom, they decided, was the place for her to blossom, the place where she could build a network of drug sellers and users, a second empire of depravity and extortion. She accepted the challenge with typical obsessive fervour. Demanding only the support of an onsite support officer and freedom of decision-making, Daria took off for her next adventure.

She had specifically chosen Familie Odin friend Alex Barber, son of an English father and Romanian mother. He was bi-national, careful, cunning resourceful and relaxed about stress. Alex had inherited a Cotswold stone farmhouse some ten miles north of Banbury, which he used as a base for his distribution of epicurean specialities to hotels, restaurants and foody pubs. Alex combined this with a regime of burglary and car theft, usually to order, and had built a group of efficient thieves, thugs and hot shoe drivers. At the end of a clutch of cable and fibre broadband feeds, plus a powerful wi-fi network, Alex had a computer installation that would make most tech companies envious.

It had been almost by accident that Alex became an IT player. One of his clients, a Chinese restaurant in Birmingham, had invited him to dinner, during which a conversation about social media fakery came up. His host, Anglo-Chinese Huw Chang, told Alex that there was a lot of money to be made facilitating fake posts and messaging and that he could act as an intermediary if Alex wanted.

Alex wanted.

He converted some farm outbuildings into small flats, hired

some cheap, motivated university IT dropouts, all dark web, Tor and social media experts, equipped his expansive cellars with sophisticated IT equipment and plied his ware via Huw Chang. Huw came up with the goods and Alex was soon regularly creating and re-posting or handling hundreds of thousands of posts and messages on behalf of customers from or connected with ROC. To his delight and amusement, Alex was also able to offer services to Russian, Iranian and Pakistani customers too; he was particularly non-partisan when money was involved.

Hacking was a natural extension of Alex's burgeoning IT interests. One of his flat tenants suggested it, and Alex held a weekend house party for hacking enthusiasts known to his social media employees. Six of them didn't leave. They would be a no-risk investment, they promised, as they would 'transfer' sufficient funds to pay themselves ten times over in the first week.

Alex had known Familie Odin for some time. It started with the innocent import of foods and wines from the Chisinau purveyor. His relationship grew when one of his hackers told Alex he'd found a way into a massive farm in Chisinau, ostensibly the legitimate communication server for his Moldovan goods supplier. Wisely choosing not to threaten the Familie Odin, Alex offered his added-value services and thereby created another significant business stream and even more substantial income. Daria had known Alex for some time after he had flown over to Chisinau to see the operation for himself and to discuss future expansions. She liked him and, as far as she could, felt him to be trustworthy. Most of all, his relaxed attitude made him amenable and malleable, and Daria knew instinctively how to use him. Alex liked Daria too but didn't trust her and wasn't prepared to be her servant. Somewhere in the middle of this clash of determined egos, there was an easy, often happy relationship of mutual benefit and healthy wariness.

Daria's timing had been difficult for Alex and his operators. Covid; its source, its effects, masks, social distancing, vaccination, governmental measures, health service responses, conspiracy, mind control, serum chips, sterilisation, ethnic targeting, political destabilisation, so many topics, so many posts, so much disinformation to spread, Covid was very time and tech-hungry but a massive boon to Alex's income. The pandemic had become a misinfodemic. Alex's units played their part by placing some of the hundreds of millions, perhaps billions, of fake posts driven mainly by China, Russia and Iran and willing national subversives and fanatics. If Alex felt any guilt at the implications of his units' web of destructive mendacity, it was assuaged when his hackers noted that redneck American networks and international xenophobic groups were busy dishing out a tsunami of anti-China and anti-anti-vaxxer posts too.

Alex's team streamlined the activity to make more free time by aggregating messages by classification and matching them to the bots and spider keyword triggers for automatic posting. The operators used this released time to concentrate on the Chisinau crisis.

For the first time in many years, Alex felt tense and preoccupied. He had a good idea of what was happening but didn't know enough to have the control he needed or to provide any degree of safety for Daria. There was going to be blood, he knew that much. Alex's immorality had strict limits, and his sense of self-preservation was acute. Flooding a world of stupid, gullible people with transparent make-believe was one thing, ending a human life was quite another, especially if the trail of guilt might come close to his front door. It was when one of his favourite dropouts told him that an unexpected intrusion into both the Chisinau centres and, possibly, a hit on their own unit had been picked up and that it led back to the USA and what looked like investigative security agencies that Alex felt a chill of anxiety. He wouldn't give up on Daria but, he thought, 'when shit comes to shove, my life comes first'.

19

Gary and Daria drove back to The Royal George with Brian trailing them in the van.

"What are we going to do with big boy then? Are we keeping him until tomorrow?"

"We need him, I think," replied Daria. "I see if we can get him room in hotel."

Gary was uneasy about this idea. He was still feeling paranoid about the quickie bet and his sore thigh and aching groin were urging him to get Daria into the bedroom as soon as possible. He didn't want a burly interloper frustrating his needs. Gary's paranoia about his relationship with Daria, his unwanted new role as mobster's moll hitman, his feelings of inadequacy, his suspicion of being used and controlled were all increasing, as his paranoia always did when he'd been drinking too much alcohol. He wanted to tell Daria to book Brian into a b&b instead, but he knew he'd be derided. Happily for Gary, the matter resolved itself.

"Brian, I get you room in hotel, you must stay to tomorrow for us."

"Tell you what, darlin, if you ain't in the room, I don't want it, I hate these flash fuckin places, feel uncomfortable don't I, me, I'll sleep in the van and all you gotta do is buy me breakfast in the morning, ok?"

"Is good Brian, you keep watch on us too, yes? Who comes, who goes if suspicious, you call me."

"Call you or nudge you darlin' your choice."

Daria gave him a stare of pure ice and walked back to the hotel, with Gary, seething again, following two steps behind.

Daria slammed the bedroom door behind Gary. He looked

shocked and quizzical at the same time.

"You laugh at Daria?"

"No, no, not at all, it's just that you look very cross," replied Gary, reaching for a bottle of wine from the hotel room 'fridge.

As he poured two glasses, he felt a sudden, vicious clamping from behind and his testicles throbbed with pain.

"I show you cross; I show you funny, you do what Daria tells, or it will be bad for you, very much hurt."

Gary gulped his wine, his head spinning with arousal, his trousers poking forward almost comically. She pushed him backwards onto the bed and jumped over him, her body over his face, suffocating him. Daria inflicted the perfect ratio of pain and torment, pleasure and frustration. As she squirmed and wriggled, she knew she needed to climax, not just physically but mentally too. This time she'd let him explode in ecstasy too. He'd be even more hers for the bidding.

It was no marathon. In less than three minutes, they both sighed with relief, eyes closed and breathing heavily. Gary needed another glass of wine; Daria felt a degree of satisfaction but, lurking in her subconscious was another appetite, a visceral hunger for something more fundamental, something more stimulating, something more deadly. Gary felt a mixture of euphoria and apprehension. Daria had been becoming more dominating, and more sadistic since they first made love. He enjoyed a certain amount of pleasure-pain, of course, but he was beginning to worry that Daria's pleasure in inflicting pain was exceeding his tolerance and beyond his enjoyment. He had another glass of wine and headed for the shower while Daria lay motionless on the bed, her eyes distant and dark.

As the water refreshed him and soothed the hurting bits, he heard her phone.

"Is Daria," he heard.

Then he heard her speak again in a voice so cold, so inhuman, so ruthless that he felt alarmed,

"In bar, yes, one hour. We will be there. How you get my number?"

She made a simple appointment sound like a death sentence. Perhaps it would be for someone.

In his farmyard apartment, Max hit the red button on his mobile, no point in hiding his identity behind a throw-away phone this time. He had been given Daria's number by one of his Alliance team who had been intercepting Alex's traffic ever since Harvey had identified the route. Alex had, unthinkingly, included her number and Brian's own phone in one of his reports to the Chisinau Familie Odin Centres. Max hadn't admitted this to Daria, he told her that he had simply asked the hotel receptionist for it. In her anger, Daria had not questioned this transparent fib. He lifted the lid on his laptop and saw the message he wanted. It was from Art and said, 'understood and done'.

Max smiled to himself, feeling less panic-stricken and more confident than when the possibility of him being attacked had first become apparent. He had Duggie as close cover, and he now believed he had the two sunglasses riding shotgun too. Dan and Jo were hidden away in safety and Sue and Indira were so well hidden even he didn't know where they were. If he'd planned it right, if Art had made the required arrangements, the next few hours would be decisive.

"You all set mate?"

"Set like concrete Max," replied Duggie, "solid and unbreakable!"

"You're getting lyrical, Dug, all this talk of murder and kidnap; it's bringing out the artist in you."

"Fuck off," said Duggie amiably, feeling more complete and fulfilled than ever before. If he died now, he'd die a happy man.

"Happy with the plan?"

"Yep."

Max fired up his fast Audi, its rorty burble making him feel strong. Perhaps a car really is an extension of manhood, he thought as the driven four wheels scrabbled briefly on the gravel under the force of acceleration.

"Bloody boy racer," thought Duggie as he selected first gear in his more modest Ford and followed on at a more sedate pace.

By the time Duggie reached the hotel car park, Max's car was parked and empty. Duggie selected a distant corner behind a garden equipment store at the far end of the hotel's accessible grounds and tucked his car away as far out of sight as he could manage. He wasn't sure why he was taking such a precaution; it was becoming a habit. 'Call me fucking 007', thought Duggie, amusing himself no end. Duggie walked slowly and purposefully towards the hotel, pausing to admire the Healy again.

Early for the meeting, Max looked around the bar. It was empty apart from two half-full Paris goblets on a table with two chairs but no people. His searching eyes looked for a seat with specific attributes. He found what he wanted, a chair against the bar's back wall and without a line of sight to a window, just in case of a sniper. From his selected seat, he could see the bar's entrances and exits, the toilet doors and the bar flap. The table would easily accommodate six people or more, but he needed only half of that capacity for him, the girl and her man.

Duggie strolled into the bar with an uncharacteristic swagger. He took no notice of Max but patted his jacket pocket meaningfully. He picked a table at the far end of the bar, and he too could see the entrances and Max's table; he could also see the window and its view.

The barman appeared and provided table service for both Duggie and Max. As he delivered their drinks, both sparkling water flavoured with elderflower cordial, a large, scruffy man wandered in from the garden door. Max recognised him immediately as the man he'd seen earlier with the woman Daria and her faithful Gary Watson. Brian called loudly for a pint of bitter and sat on a barstool, his back to Duggie, his eyes on Max.

Bravado or hubris pondered Max as he ventured a smile at Brian. A flat, implacable gaze was all that Max had in return. He felt the visual connection had put him in the ascendancy, but he wasn't sure why he felt it to be so. Wishing he'd ordered something stronger, Max sipped his drink and composed himself. He had an outline plan but couldn't know how the evening would unfold. 'Tap dance it, kid', he told himself.

Duggie watched the barman busy himself doing nothing obvious behind the bar. A shadowy movement caught the corner of his eye. He looked towards the window and saw, he thought, two dark-suited men walk slowly by.

Daria made an entrance. Stepping out like a well-drilled soldier, she marched in, taller in high stiletto heels. She exuded confidence and authority in her dark blue slim-fitting suit and high-necked white shirt, partially concealing a pearl choker. Her intense, cold blue eyes accentuated by film-style mascara, her hair high and cascading down behind her neck, Daria had dressed for the occasion. She looked wonderful and she knew it.

Brian gaped, Duggie followed her every move and Max, looking directly at her, couldn't help thinking 'bugger me, I'd have some of that'.

Playing for an early advantage, Daria offered an elegantly postured hand.

"Daria Duca, Chisinau Food and Wine Specialists."

"Max Golby, Onetelcall I.T. Security Specialist."

They shook hands and Max felt an electricity-like shock as he touched her skin. He understood in an instance how this woman could make most men do anything she asked of them.

Attempting to support his partner, Gary held out his hand too.

"Gary Watson, not a specialist in anything," he grinned.

Max smiled back, slightly disarmed for a moment by Gary's easy charm. Max also noticed Gary's red, watery eyes and caught the aroma of wine on his breath.

"It's a pleasure to meet you, Gary, thank you for coming. Please, both of you, sit down. What would you like to drink?"

From his distant seat, Duggie was amused by the theatrical politeness of the meeting. Brian stared in confusion. 'If you're going to kill this fucker, why bother to be nice to him?' he wondered.

The drinks arrived while the three sat and arranged themselves.

"Za vashe zdorovie," said Max, clinking his glass against Daria's and then Gary's. He watched as Daria sipped and Gary glugged.

"I'll pop another in the pipeline Gary," smiled Max, now knowing he'd got yet one more card in his hand of trumps.

"Oh, thanks mate, cheers," said Gary. Daria shot an evil glance at him.

"Enough of this English good manners," she said assertively, "we not here for chitchat. You know why we are here, we are not your friends, not your cheers, and we will have what we must have, you violate us, you pay. That is all to say."

Detecting a hint of nervousness behind Daria's sternness, Max replied, "Actually, old girl, that isn't all that needs to be said. There's much more to be said and it must be said to both of you."

Gary spoke up because he thought he should. "Look here, mate, you're bloody lucky to be here at all, don't start messing about with us; this isn't a game, you know."

Daria turned to see Brian stand up, looking as aggressive as he could which, he knew, was intimidating even to the bravest and most pugnacious opponent. Allowing Max time to absorb this scenario, Daria turned back and smiled coldly at him. Max nodded towards the far end of the bar. Daria turned again; behind Brian, she saw a small, insignificant man looking directly at her. She was about to laugh in superiority when Duggie revealed the barrel of his pistol from under his jacket.

"No Daria, this is no game."

Infuriated at being out-manoeuvred again, Daria hissed, "Your little man with gun no threat here. Your life, Mr Golby, and the life of your colleagues belong to me. You have forfeited right to breathe. Tonight, will not end well for you, no matter you feel you have won a point, you will lose fight."

Daria nodded at Brian who winked back in acknowledgement. He rushed out of the room, towards the car park and his van.

"You are two, we are more. You have little pop gun, we have arms. You feel brave, we are fearless, you think you can fight, we know you can't. Tonight, you will leave with me, and we go where you won't come back. That is fact. Tell your poodle to get back in basket or he die where he sits. Don't for a moment think we won't do what we say, killing is natural to us, your little man means nothing. He will lose his life for nothing, and you will be responsible for his death if you don't give order now. Brian will have him in sights by now, nothing you can do to stop him. I raise my hand and wave, Brian shoot. Will not miss head. Nothing else to say."

"Before you kill my friend, there are a couple of facts of ours that I should share with you," said Max so calmly he amazed himself. "Your two centres in Chisinau are already compromised. If my friend and I die here, nothing will change; your operation is bust. Your communication platform for your drug dealing here in the UK is now ours, we can post on it, break it, whatever we want. You have lost it, and your associates will seek their revenge on you and your family for what you've let happen. Your entire UK operation is exposed, and we have all the details, all the people, all the drug import routes, all the distributors, the lot. They are being arrested as we speak, starting with your chum Alex."

Max immediately regretted over-playing his hand. He could

see that she already knew that the Moldovan centres had been accessed by the frown that flicked across her brow but her face relaxed when he suggested imminent arrests; she knew that was a lie.

"Even if what you say is true, which it isn't, it is more western lies, you still die today. You and your little man, you die, no choice. Whatever you think you have, you won't have. We are too clever to be caught by you, Familie Odin reaches around world, you may be inconvenience for a short time, but you won't stop, you won't defeat Familie Odin."

"OK, Daria, but before we go, I'd just like to address Gary. You see, I know you've brainwashed the poor fellow into believing he is some sort of hitman. I can see how he'd fall for you, how he'd do what you tell him to do but does he know the full story, Daria? Does he know that once he's killed me and the others on your shopping list that he'll be the next one to die? Does he know he's expendable to you? Does he believe he'll live a life of luxury and bliss with you ever after? Does he? Do you Gary?"

"Don't come it with me, matey-boy. I know every trick in the book. I've conned and connived my way through life, and I know how to survive; you can't put a wobbler into me 'cos I don't wobble. Daria and me, we are the same sort of people, we are winners in a battle of the best. If we kill, we kill because we have to and because we can, without remorse, without hesitation. She and I have been through lots already and we won't be divided by your pathetic attempts to undermine us. If I had any doubts about finishing you off, well, I don't anymore."

Gary finished speaking, his face red and sweaty, his hands visibly shaking. He picked the second and third drinks Max had ordered and swallowed them in quick succession. He indicated to the barman to bring another.

"Met in a rehab, didn't you Gary, you and Daria? Except Daria's not an alcoholic, but you are. Look at you now, you couldn't pick up a gun, aim and pull the trigger; you just couldn't physically manage it. You are six doubles in already, on top of what you've drunk in your room and you're craving more. Your hands will shake again in minutes unless you get your refill. I suggest, mate, that you put aside any ideas of shooting me and listen to what I have to say instead."

"Fuck off, I'm fine, and I'm not listening to your bollocks anymore." Gary held out the flat of his hand to show how steady he was; it trembled and shook.

"Ok, Gary, don't listen to me. You probably wouldn't believe what I say, you are too far gone in drunken lust. So, how about reading, eh? How about I show you absolute proof from your team of comrades that you are as valuable to them as a day-old turd?"

"You can't prove anything. I'm no turd, but, dead man talking, you are full of shit."

Max could see Brian's silhouette in the half-light of the window, he could see a dark, long shape of a rifle barrel. He could see that Duggie had seen it too. Duggie was looking calm but pale. His hand was still on the butt of his Beretta, ready to shoot if he had to. He could see Daria's hand twitching, straining against her control to signal the fire order to Brian.

"Let's just stay calm for a moment longer, shall we? Gary, mate, I might just prove to be the best mate you've ever had. Read this."

Max opened his phone on the message Harvey had pinged to him - the copy of Alex's message stating incontrovertibly that Gary would be disposed of the moment he had done his work. There could be no doubt.

"I don't believe that shit," said Gary, now looking desperate. The barman bought his next drink while Gary stood up to look threatening. He downed the drink and sat again.

"You don't eh Gary? Well, I thought you'd think we faked it, so, please, scroll down those messages, the messages your chum Alex has been sending to his Moldovan masters, read them and ask yourself how could we have faked these private, accurate details, details you know to be true and accurate and which prove beyond any doubt that these are the real thing."

Gary scrolled, looking more wide-eyed, perspiration running in rivulets down his face. He looked at Daria like a Labrador about to be beaten.

"Daria, my lover, my friend, my girl. Tell me this is fake, tell me it's another con from these bastards. Tell me."

"Gary, Gary, there may have been talk about you being danger after you kill, but that was before now, now is different, now you trust me and do what we have to do and we will go back home together and live the way we planned, you know this, Gary, look at me and know it."

"Arrant bullshit, Gary, surely even you can see she's trying it on, trying to save herself now because it is you two who are in danger now, not me. Think about it Gary, you may get out of this with your life yet but if you believe her and not what you've read and know to be true, the likelihood is that it will be you who dies tonight."

Gary's alcohol-befuddled mind collapsed in confusion. Tears were adding to the streams of sweat on his face. He stood and walked unsteadily to the bar. He ordered two more doubles and drank them urgently. The booze worked in minutes. Gradually, his hands stopped shaking so much, his facial blush subsided, and his cheeks dried. Two more doubles and Gary felt in control of himself again.

The barman indicated to Max that he wouldn't serve Gary again. Daria saw the signal and knew that the meeting was reaching its apotheosis. She had some decisions to make, and she had to calm herself to make the right decisions. When Gary walked to the bar, she had been on the point of ordering the shooting. As he stood, swaying slightly, downing his drinks, Daria felt nothing but revulsion. Fleetingly, she remembered their first meeting, how she felt attracted to him and believed she could mould him into being a useful lieutenant and an on-demand lover. He had been callous and libidinous, the perfect combination for her.

Her thoughts turned to Brian. Brian the brawn, Brian the yob. Useless, brainless and deceitful, a typical bully-coward, she knew, and not to be relied on for anything, especially if duty vied with self-survival. He'd run out without hesitation. But he might still have some purpose before he capitulated. She was, she concluded, in a tight spot. It wasn't what she'd planned but she'd been in sticky situations before, and she told herself, she could still win, she could still maintain the honour of Familie Odin.

As Gary sagged onto the barstool previously occupied by Brian, Daria knew it was time to be precipitous. She raised her hand and waved the instruction for Brian to fire his rifle. She closed her eyes and flinched in anticipation of the carnage her gesture would unleash. Nothing. No explosive sound, no scream of agony, no tumult of panic, no shrieks for police. Peace; only melodic background music could be heard.

She opened her eyes to see Max smiling smugly. She turned her eyes to the window where Brian's sniping position should have been, searching for his shape in the half-light, but saw none, no shape, no rifle barrel. He had been there, she had seen him, but he had gone, disappeared. Daria was confused and disconcerted. Max's knowing grin was a triumph of obfuscation. The moment Daria raised her hand, Max saw Duggie whip out his pistol and expected to see Brian's bulk fill the window frame as his rifle's bullet smashed through to hit... who? Duggie? Gary? Him?

Brian was confused too. He saw Daria's hand begin to rise, he readied himself for a fairground pot-shot at the selected duck and then felt a mind-numbing armlock around his throat and a bone-breaking blow to his right arm, his trigger arm. He had wanted to howl and yell, but some material that smelled like a hospital had been rammed into his mouth. His sudden confusion gave way to blackness as the chloroform-ether-soaked rag took effect. Duggie, courageous now in his role of bodyguard, had seen Brian's silhouette bend and collapse before it disappeared sideways, like a stage exit. He guessed someone had jumped the thug but didn't bother to think about it too much; his reaction was to train his pistol on Daria.

Gary remained unaware of the drama behind him. The barman was more aware of the action but could not understand what was happening in his bar. He was perplexed and rattled; he needed a drink and hit the whiskey optic several times, filling his glass. He caught an imploring look from Gary and, despite his dislike of drunks, gave him another double-double too.

"How quickly things change, eh Daria?"

"If only lies you tell me were not lies, you would be with upper hand. But I know you lie. You might not die tonight, but you will die soon. Daria always succeeds, you will see."

"You overstate your position, young lady. Your trained killer is now a drunken wreck and your goon with a gun seems to have done a runner. You're on your own and have a pistol pointing at you. Not going so well for you, I'd say."

"You not stop me, I leave now, your English reserve and good manners, you won't shoot me in public, you not attack woman in public. You will let me walk out of bar and you not stop me. You lie about police. I know you not involve police now or to get Alex. Your police have nothing to handle this fight; you have nothing. You can have Gary and the man out there; they nothing, not important, I have power and resource you not know or understand. You think you win; you not win, you make sure of your death. That is fact of tonight."

She stood up, composed and elegant again, and strutted slowly, erect and proud, from the bar towards the lift and the sanctuary of her room.

Max tapped a rapid message into his phone: 'Art, gone as planned, send in transport'.

A couple of minutes later, a professional-looking man, mid-thirties and wearing a well-cut business suit, strode into the bar. He needed no instruction, no niceties. He approached Gary, who gazed at him with unfocussed blank eyes and meekly allowed the man to take him by the arm and lead him from the bar to the hotel's exit to the car park. Max stood and walked to the window. He could see two more men, both in overalls similar to paramedics. They were carrying a stretcher on which lay a body covered with a blanket. It was, he knew, the inert Brian being taken away.

"Come on, Duggie, I think we are safe now; let's get the fuck away from here. It's late and I'm hungry."

Duggie concurred. He followed his friend, wondering what on earth would happen next.

20

In her room, Daria fell onto the bed. She wanted to cry but she hadn't cried since she was ten years old and wouldn't give in now. From her covert activities in various rehabs, she had seen and learned the dangers of drink and drugs but, at times like this, she could understand why people resorted to them so readily. She opened her Louis Vuitton vanity case and found the small bottle of her favourite slivovitz. One slug would help, and she'd still have a clear head, she thought. She felt comforted by the warmth of the strong spirit but was still in turmoil, her thoughts tumbled around in her mind. It reminded her of what many alcoholics referred to as their washing machine heads. She explored her vanity case again and found the small silver vial-like canister she wanted. It was nitrous oxide, her hippy-crack.

She had discovered the effects of laughing gas when the food and wine company gave away nitrous oxide-powered corked bottle openers as a promotion. One of the Chechen escapees who worked in the Chisinau food and wine export department had shown her how to inhale the gas; she had felt an immediate euphoria and relaxation, along with a fit of giggles. She knew a puff from a small canister would give her the instant mental assuagement she so urgently needed after her clash with Max.

Daria let herself revel in the solace that the gas and drink afforded her for half an hour. The effects diminished, but her iron will and resolve were fully restored. She was already forming plans for her next move. She picked up her phone and hit her Verivoip app, an encrypted voice and video link to Alex. His face appeared on her screen in seconds; he looked distraught. She put her finger to her lips to suggest their link may not be as secure as the system provider claimed its encryption to be. As video was less likely to be analysed by snoopers, Daria pointed at herself and then at Alex; she made steering wheel movements and held up three fingers against her watch. Alex nodded in understanding and confirmation.

At that time, from late night to early morning, it took Daria only two hours to hustle her hire car from Olderbury to Alex's Cotswold farmhouse; she was exhausted when she arrived. Alex rushed out to greet her and, seeing her failing physical state, helped her from the car and guided her to her bedroom as she leaned against him to stay upright. He gave her time to get into bed and returned carrying a large brandy which Daria drank like a child having bedtime milk.

Ten hours later, Daria awoke, alarmed at seeing the mid-morning sun glowing through the heavy curtains of the farmhouse bedroom. As she was washing in the old-fashioned bedroom basin, there was a knock on her door. One of Alex's team of young techies carried in a tray of steaming dark coffee and a couple of pain-au-chocolate.

"Here you are, babe," he announced with a re-assuringly friendly manner and not intending any over-familiarity, "Alex says he hopes you slept ok and to meet him in the basement when you are ready; you go downstairs, through the kitchen and it's the big oak door on the left of the big window."

Feeling refreshed and fortified by her coffee and sweet bread, Daria soon found Alex, surrounded by screens and eager young faces.

"Hey Daria, we have traffic like you wouldn't believe," said Alex by way of greeting; Daria approved of this no-nonsense approach.

"Uncle Alexandru," she felt the need to emphasise the close family connection and to establish her position in front of the onlooking geeks, "how much you know of what happened last night?"

"All I can say, my dear, is that if we had a field full of fans, you wouldn't see them for fertilizer. It looks like your Onetelcall targets are just figureheads in what is a concerted attack on both of our centres. From what we can see, several other really big farms, factories and disrupter networks; they've all been opened up by a US organisation and the security agencies we spotted yesterday."

"I see," said Daria, "are we completely blown? Is it disaster?"

"It's carnage ok, but we are not finished yet. I'll tell you now, Daria, I'll stay here supporting you and doing all I can, but if the bastards who are trying to break us get any closer, I'm saving my skin without a doubt, you understand me? I'll save yours too, but we may have to cut and run; I, for one, am not getting caught or arrested or worse, I haven't come this far to end up in prison or in a graveyard."

"Don't talk defeat to me, Alex," replied Daria, shunning the family connection, "you not run, I not run, we fight, as long as we have breath, we fight, not lost yet and we can recover, we have to recover."

Alex looked at Daria, impressed by her indomitability. "I'm not running yet and, yeah, we'll fight, but we've got to be a bit cleverer than we have been. I suspect whatever happened last night shows that all too clearly; what did happen anyway, where's Brian?"

"I don't know, I saw him through window, I saw his shape, I saw his long gun barrel and I thought I saw flash of reflection from his gunsight but when I gave him signal to attack, in the way we had agreed, nothing happened, he was gone and not seen since."

"And Gary?"

Daria's implacable expression became a look that combined anger and sadness.

"Hah, Gary. I left him in hotel bar with the pig Max and his lapdog. I am ashamed, Uncle, I have been weak and not used best judgement. When he told me, in Harbour House, that he was special and different, I thought he was; I thought I could make him into something, a man, a proper man who would do good for family and who would be good for me. I was wrong. I was so wrong. He not have the strength in head, not have the strength in spirit, only spirit he has comes from bottle. He is beyond being man and now I despise him. He should be dead, already he is dead to me."

"But Daria, if Max has got him, you can be sure he'll get all the information about us out of Gary; he wouldn't need torture, just a big bottle of brandy would do it."

"Is true Uncle Alexandru, he sell his mother for a drink, I know this is true. Probably Max has Gary and Brian and will try to find as much of our secret as he can, but I think we not worry too much. Gary, his brain is always drunk and Brian, he has no brain at all; Gary knows a bit about our, um, distribution business around rehabs but not enough for me to worry, he now knows names, places, how it all is organised, so not worry at all. I think Brian knows what day is but not much else, is that right?"

Alex smiled despairingly, "Brian is great at what he does, drive and intimidate but not much else; even when I've explained why I'm asking him to do something, he doesn't understand. He can't tell anyone anything of much use, and, of course, his pride won't let him say anything to anyone who thinks they can force him to speak."

"I am not sure, Brian, is, I see, a bully and a coward. If he is frightened, he will give in like little girl; no, little girls have bravery, he'll give in like whipped puppy. But he knows nothing; I am sure he doesn't know what he knows anyway, he is not worry to us."

Alex smiled to himself at Daria's intolerance; he also felt a nag of concern. Could Brian tell his captors too much about the secrets of his farm?

"Let us not waste time on those two, Uncle, we have more important work to do. How much have you told home? Did you make report after last night?"

"Yeah, we've been on the private Tor Onion comms a lot since your video call. As I said, they have a shit-load of problems of their own right now, after all the trouble the Onetelcall exposure has caused, so all I've told them is that all the spies, your targets, are still alive and that our plans to stop them in their tracks have, er, not worked. Word is from Chisinau that we shouldn't give up, but more important than straightforward revenge deaths, they say, is finding out as much as possible about the size of the organisation which is busting our organisation open so easily and then to do whatever we can to destroy, not only the people but their infrastructure too."

"Yes," nodded Daria, "I could have guessed they would say something like that. What are they doing to help us? Are they sending me some men, some equipment? What is their strategy?"

"Zilch, girl, fucking zero, I'm afraid. You are on your own- that is we are on our own, but let me say again, I'm right behind you until my life is in danger and then I'm gone, vapour, so should you be too, by the way."

Daria made an explosive tutting sound. "My life is Familie Odin, is my family, my life my DNA, I not turn away, not run away, not fear for life because without family I have no life to live. You run, you turn your back on those who trust you, those who have made you what you are now, you be traitor if you must, not Daria, I'll not be vapour with you, or for you."

"Ok, Daria, ok, I'm no quitter and you know that after all these years. Just saying I'm not a suicide merchant, that's all, live to fight another day and all that."

"So, what have we got? We have not got your Brian; we have not got his car or his rifle. I know what we haven't got, but what have we got that I can go to war with?"

"War?" he scorned. "Going to war? You, me against God knows who or what; a little Quixotic, wouldn't you say, a bit Alamo, a bit Rourke's Drift. I'm all for heroic action, even on long odds, but you are seriously telling me you want to go into battle against an enemy whose strength you have no way of knowing?"

"Yes, Alex, that is what I'm saying, and I repeat, what have we got?"

"Tell you what, shall I call you David? You tell me what sort of battle plan you have to conquer Goliath and I'll tell you if and how I can arm you and what back-up we can muster... Custer."

"I am going to get to Max. I am going to talk; I am going to find out what he knows. I am going to find way of making him offer he says 'yes' to and trap him one way or another. When I know what he has, what Onetelcall has and what their plans are, I shall destroy their machines, their operation, I will destroy as family tells me."

"Well, it's a sort of start to a plan, I suppose. I can give you a Snake-Slayer Derringer; it's very small, very lethal, you can hide it in your handbag or down your knickers, anywhere, but it only has two shots; still, it could be a lifesaver. I can give you some secure 'phones, some radio kits, like trackers, bugs, cameras and so on, whatever you want, and, if I've understood your mission of destruction correctly, I can get some very special EPX-1 explosive, detonators and all the kit plus, my girl, and this is a big plus, me because I know how to handle it without blowing myself up when I'm still ten miles away from the target."

"You are volunteering to be bomb man?"

"Yep, I suppose I am."

"I have hire car, I have room in hotel, I not book out yet, I have big knowledge of men like Max bastard Golby and I have my mind. Is unbeatable, yes?"

"Yes, unbeatable, I'm sure, but how about a helping hand? I've got a stash of fentanyl, a few drops of that in his drink and he'll be so out of it he'll tell you anything you want to know."

Alex and Daria enjoyed a moment of laughter, buoyed for the first time since she arrived, by some positive thoughts and determination to act.

"Now, Alex, there is need to communicate with family again.

We must know what information they have about what outsider knowledge there is of intrusions and what effect news is having on our business. We must know what they are doing, know to counteract effects and to secure systems again against more spies and their tame hackers and do-goody geeks."

"Yes, that makes sense; I'll get on it now and, if I may suggest Madam Napoleon, you start figuring out how you intend to make contact with Golby again, what you are going to say and how you are going to extract any information from him."

"Not Napoleon, no exile for me because I think I already have plan for this Alex, it is oldest plan in world, I think, but it works well for Daria. I see it work, I grow up with it working for family and I think, when bastard Golby first saw me, he liked what he saw." Daria posed tartily to make her point.

"Well, girl, as an uncle, I can say that nobody does it better, Ms Bond. How could he resist eh? He stands no chance."

"This not me being too much me, me, me. This is proper plan and thinking. We know, don't we, that bastard Golby is man alone, he likes girls, but he has not one of his own, he has needs and desires like all men, I know these, and I can speak to his needs I think."

21

Gary felt terrible. It was a feeling he knew well. It meant that he had drunk himself insensible again; something he had promised himself he wouldn't do, something he'd learnt how to avoid during his time in rehab. He felt as though he'd not so much fallen off the wagon as leapt from a moving train. Dry mouth, sweaty, shaky, sick, panicky, confused, fearful, he attempted to gather his thoughts, but none combined to offer coherent answers to the where, why, how, when and what questions in his mind.

He propped himself up on one elbow; strange bed, strange room, familiar though. He looked around. The room was just like the one he'd… and memory of what had happened began to trickle back through the fug. Across the room, he could see another bed, and another person and more memories came to him. The other body was that oafy oik Brian. Gary felt his bowels tremor and groin shrivel as his mind showed him pictures of the preceding night. His head found the pillow again and he closed his eyes in some confused reality escape attempt.

He heard Brian move, moan loudly and then shout, "What the fuck's going on? Where am I? Fuck it, what are you doing here, arsehole? Where are we? What's fuckin' happening?"

Gary opened his eyes and saw Brian sitting on the edge of his bed, staring straight at him with unconcealed malevolence. His torpid mind attempted an answer.

"Dunno."

This answer didn't satisfy Brian and Gary watched him stand up, walk across the room and kick the door hard and repeatedly until it began to fracture. Then it opened. As the door swung, a fist appeared, it connected with Brian's left cheek, and he staggered back towards Gary's bed where he buckled. A man in a suit, who Gary recognised from his vague recollections of the night before, followed the fist into the room. Accompanying the suit were two men in medical overalls. The two men manoeuvred Brian to an upright bedroom chair and stood on either side of him.

"I am Trevor," announced the man in the suit, looking meaningfully at Gary and Brian in turn, "these are my associates, and you will be our guests until you have answered all of my questions. If you don't answer, we will be here for a long time, and it will be very painful for you. You can see that you are in a hotel room, and you might think that if you shout, some help will come and save you. Don't please allow yourself to make any noise; it will end up being even more painful for you. Is that clear?"

Gary nodded. He also squirmed, feeling an intense need to urinate.

Brian growled, "Fuck off, you fucking tosser."

Without word or sign, one of the medical men stepped behind the chair, grabbed both of Brian's arms and pulled them back while the other stuffed a Sorbo rubber ball in his mouth. Silenced and with arms tied painfully behind the chairback, Brian was subdued and, although his eyes glinted with malice, his head and body slumped, indicating to his captors a mental capitulation.

Gary gaped at Brian's suppression, whose crotch was now very damp with leaking urine.

"Gary, we will start with you. If you try to arouse any attention by shouting, screaming or any means at all, you will be hurt and we will hurt your friend here too; I don't think he'll thank you for that, so be very careful. Clear?"

Gary may have been the instigator of intimidation against others in the past, but this was the first time he truly understood the power of threatened physical agony.

Trevor Selby had amassed a lot of dislikes in his thirty-six years. He didn't like weakness; he didn't like bullies and he didn't like violence. In his job as a special operations fixer for international legal practices, he came across many people he disliked, which made his work a great deal easier. His two associates, Clive and Malcolm, were partners in arms and in life. They had met during basic training in the army, where their toughness and aggression masked their innermost emotions. They exceeded expectations in combat roles and saw action in both Iraq and Afghanistan. At the end of their last tour, they realised they couldn't maintain the charade anymore and resigned. After six years of fighting, they had seen terrible violence and knew little about anything else. They resolved to use their skills for good wherever possible and, after a skirmish where they had taken on and beaten a homophobic gang, the couple acquired notoriety as 'The Gay Rangers'.

For all his dislikes, Trevor didn't dislike gay men, he did, however, dislike those who disliked gay men. He had met the couple after a court hearing where Clive and Malcolm appeared for the prosecution after they had snared an anti-gay thug in action, beating up a young musician. Trevor had been asked to protect the victim for the day and when the court allowed the thugs to walk away with a hefty fine, Clive and Malcolm had a word with him on his way home. The louts ended up in hospital; there were no witnesses to his assault. Trevor approved no end and invited the two men to join him in his varied, justifiable and profitable work.

Trevor and 'The Gay Rangers' had a reputation for sound judgement, reliability and discretion in the UK and overseas, as far as New York and Arthur Pincher. They were the go-to resource to provide the services that Max had requested. They were used to working alone and the two Rangers had been surprised to find Jesus and Angelo stalking the same prey. Dressed in their ambulance-men outfits, Clive and Malcolm had stayed in the shadows, watching Brian from a safe distance, when they saw the two burly men, wearing sunglasses at night, also appearing to be following him.

When Brain made his move to fire, the two big men in suits were on him before his eye could meet the rifle's sight and he was subdued, silenced and floored in a second. Angelo and Jesus had intended to bind the man and leave him in the shrubbery. Waving an impromptu white flag, Malcolm's handkerchief, the Rangers approached the suits and in just a few words agreed that Brian would remain in their custody and Angelo and Jesus could leave to pursue their next course of action, which would be to protect Max and Duggie.

Trevor's abhorrence of weakness was at its peak as he started questioning the shaking, slightly malodorous Gary. He moved slowly to stand behind him, lowered his face to inches from Gary's right ear and got to work. Although Gary could sense his inquisitor's mouth near his ear, he had to strain to hear Trevor whisper, "You will say yes or no and only yes or no to the following questions, is that clear?"

Gary wanted to nod but couldn't move. Brian wanted to yell at him, tell him not to say anything, but he couldn't speak. Trevor put a microphone on the table next to Gary and turned his recorder on.

"Do you know Daria Duca?"

"Do you know Alex Barber?"

"Do you know a farmhouse in north Oxfordshire where Alex lives?"

"Do you know about a food and wine company in Moldova?"

"Do you know about drugs being sold by that company?"

The whispered questions kept coming relentlessly as Gary almost shouted his 'yes' answers.

"So far so good," said Trevor, walking back to be face to face with the now whimpering Gary, "let's get into a bit more detail, shall we?"

Brian was thrashing about on his chair in a frantic effort to make Gary shut up. Gary was oblivious to everything except Trevor's eyes, staring into his own.

For two hours, Trevor interrogated Gary, pushing him for the minutest details, double-checking points of relevance and some of irrelevance too, to keep Gary off-balance. When he was sure he had wrung every scrap of useful information from Gary, Trevor picked him up by his shirt and threw him onto his bed. Cast aside like a sucked orange, Gary lay motionless, empty and exhausted.

Again, without a word or sign, Clive and Malcolm manhandled Brian to the room's dressing table, where they forced his hands to sit flat on the wooden surface and carefully placed G-clamps from the base of the table over each of his fingers' first interphalangeal joints. They tightened the clamps to a well-judged point of pain without injury and nodded to Trevor.

Trevor leaned nonchalantly against the end of the dressing table, adjusting his tie in the mirror, before speaking to Brain as if he were greeting an old friend.

"Thanks so much for helping us out here, Brian, I know you want to talk to me, and we'll have a grand old chat, I'm sure. And just to show how much I'm looking forward to our little natter, I'm going to ask my friends to take the ball out of your mouth. Just before they do that, I should tell you that if you try to make a noise or if you don't answer any of my questions, they will tighten one of those clamps and crush your fingers one by one."

Clive placed a small hammer by the side of Brian's left hand.

"Oh yes, thank you for reminding me," smiled Trevor at his colleague. "If you decide to be difficult, Brian, my friend here will tap each broken finger with his little hammer and if you scream in agony, as, of course, you will, well, he'll just have to tap a bit more. Hard old life, isn't it?"

Brian's bellicose bravado vanished, leaving only his grimace of fear. Trevor's dislike of bullying cowards prompted a smile of anticipation. Clive removed the Sorbo ball from Brian's mouth making him hiss with pain as his jaw muscles protested at the abuse.

"Fuckin bastards," he muttered. Clive turned the butterfly screw on Brian's left-hand little finger G-clamp one more quarter turn. Brian howled in pain.

"I told you not to make a noise," said Trevor calmly. "I told you what would happen if you made a noise now, didn't I?"

Clive turned the screw another eighth of a rotation. Brian bit his lip until it bled, silently.

"Good chap, I knew you'd want to be as helpful as possible, so let's get going then, shall we?"

After half an hour of close questioning, Trevor realised that Brian found remembering his phone number a mental challenge. He had gleaned as much as possible about Alex, the farmhouse, the people in the farmhouse, the computers in the cellar and Alex's various burglary and car-theft activities. He also discovered that Alex had built a small arsenal of guns and had a collection of surveillance equipment too. He noted this for passing on to Art as he guessed Alex might be putting all this equipment to use very soon.

Brian's fractured little finger was swollen and blue-black when the G-clamp was removed. He wanted to shriek in anguish as it was released but the thought of that small hammer kept him quiet. Clive and Malcolm guided him to the bed, where Gary was still inert and made him lie down. They then removed both Gary's and Brian's trousers, disgusted at Gary's soiled clothing, and tied their legs together in what would be described later as a compromising position. It was their little treat to themselves for a job well done.

Trevor, Clive and Malcolm left the hotel room, pulling the splintered door closed behind them. Only the sounds of Gary's sobs and Brian's groans followed them.

22

Feeling safe and reassured by what he saw as a victory, Max told Duggie to go home for the rest of the night and catch up on his sleep. Duggie was uneasy about leaving his charge unprotected, but he was exhausted, and the lure of his pillow was too strong to resist. Max, too, was spent. With his last waking breath, he set his alarms and checked the camera systems and, within seconds of that effort, was asleep and stayed that way until his phone trilled, announcing an incoming message.

We have impasse. We both fight, we both lose. Jaw jaw not war war, say your hero Churchill, why not we do that? Come to hotel at midday please. Meet and talk for best good. Txt me when arrive. D.

Max smiled to himself, imagining how much thought had gone into the psychologically appealing Churchill reference and what effort it must have taken to insert the 'please'.

"It's on-again," said Max to Duggie, "the Royal George again, twelve o'clock, you want to pop round here for a coffee or two first?"

Duggie said he'd be there in a few minutes, giving Max time to message Art and tell him about the new arrangement. Art confirmed he'd had full debriefs from all concerned about last night's events and was making appropriate arrangements for today's meeting. By all accounts, Alex had been in contact with Chisinau again but as the messages had been bouncing around the world on the Tor messaging system, he didn't yet know the content. Max felt a tinge of disquiet, about not being fully armed with the latest intelligence but knew Art was doing all he could to keep him and Duggie safe.

Back in her hotel room, Daria was preparing for round two with Max. She had an unopened bottle of Famous Grouse, sealed small bottles of water and hotel glasses, still in their closed cellophane bags. She found a crease in the cellophane of one of the glasses, sufficient to hide the tiny pin-prick hole left by her syringe.

She dressed in aroused anticipation. The thought of being an irresistible seductress excited her and the mirror confirmed her suitability for the role. Her blonde hair piled high, cascading down her back, a figure-hugging little black dress, pearl choker, and high heels, set off with skilled and dramatic make-up, with special attention to her blue eyes, all combined to make Daria feel ready for any man. Her room was made ready too. She had sprayed just a little perfume into the air, had some music playing from an easy-listening station on the hotel's DAB radio, and had hidden her microphone behind the armchair where she would invite Max to sit. Any signs that Gary had been present in the room had been eradicated; he no longer existed.

At ten minutes past twelve, Max parked in the hotel car park and Duggie resumed his previous semi-hidden lookout position. A few cars away gleamed the big Healy he coveted so much. Max sent his arrival text to Daria who responded immediately with her room number, no message, just the number that Max relayed to Duggie before striding into the hotel.

Max hadn't expected to be pre-empted by Daria; he'd planned to make the next move in his entrapment of the Chisinau gang. After receiving the text, he'd been musing about Daria's purpose. He doubted she had invited him to the hotel to kill him, kidnap him or do him any harm. There would be easier, safer ways for her to achieve any of those objectives. It must be a fact-finding mission, he thought. She needs to know who we are, what we know and what we intend to do. So did he. He'd know more about Daria and her gang by the end of this lunchtime, and have loads of info to pass on, enough to put an end to them for good and all. He knew that Chisinau was only one micro-operation in a worldwide nexus, but the damage it wrought was immeasurable and must be stopped.

He felt oddly furtive as he tapped on Daria's hotel room door.

"Mr Golby, or shall I call you Max?" Daria opened the door slowly, her most melting smile firmly in place. She quivered slightly inside when she saw Max's eyes widen and his breath catch perceptibly when he saw her. "I am flattered and honoured that, after last night, you trust and come to my room." She fixed him with prolonged eye-to-eye contact as she gestured him into the room and to the designated armchair.

"I know you have suspicions, so I make sure you see that all is above the board. You see new bottle, new water, new glasses, all ok for both of us, we drink, yes?"

Max nodded, looking around the room for any cameras or out-of-place items. Daria noisily extracted the glasses from their wrappers, cracked open the scotch and waters and poured two generous drinks, proffering a nearly-full glass to Max, which he took without question.

"Na Zdorovie," said Daria, raising her glass and chinking it against his.

"Nostrovia," he replied, wondering why he was cheering this woman, who was effectively an enemy and his killer like she was an old friend.

As she sat on the carefully positioned second armchair, obliquely opposite him, and crossed her legs slowly and knowingly, he couldn't help but watch, transfixed by her blend of attractiveness and apparent availability. Daria watched as he took a long sip from his scotch and water.

"So, Max, are we to be enemies and fight to the death or is there a more grown-up solution to our impasse?" She smiled warmly and leaned forwards as she spoke.

"I have no interest in fighting," replied Max as coolly as possible, "my only interest is in preventing the spread of misinformation, lies, propaganda and fake messages from any and all sources, most notably, in this case, the operation you and your family run in Chisinau where you peddle drugs and try to subvert the west with state-sponsored indoctrination."

"You say pretty speech, Max, and I understand you mean to be hero and fight for your right. Is easy for you in soft belly of England to have principles and do only what you think is proper. Is different, very different, in my country where we do what told or we get big trouble or death if not."

"Then let me help you, Daria. Perhaps I can get you out of the trap you are in, free you from the powers who make you and your family spread such evil influence?"

Was this the opening Daria had been waiting for? Was the fentanyl beginning to take effect? She moved forward in her chair, watching his reaction to her advance.

"If only that could be true, Max, if only you could be saviour. Brave and strong you are but you are only one man, and you cannot fight against the power of those in control in my country. It was lovely thought but is only a dream, I think. You are alone and you would need much more behind you if you take on fight for me."

Max noticed the implied invitation to describe what backup and support he had available and also recognised that Daria was turning it into a fight for her and not a battle against her organisation; he admired her manipulative skills while he finished his drink, saying nothing. Feeling warm, he stood up and walked to the window, which he opened as far as the health and safety retaining straps allowed. She appeared beside him; he could feel her thigh press against his as they stood close together. Max felt even warmer and elated at her proximity.

"But you do have soldiers in your army, don't you, Max? You had people last night fighting for you, protecting you, I saw." She moved closer still, their bodies touching from shoulder to knee, her head millimetres from his, her mouth so close to his ear.

Max could feel his body and his senses going into overdrive, his control of movement becoming weakened, and his mind becoming kaleidoscopic. The glow from the drug made Max want to love everyone, talk to everyone and be happy, especially he wanted to take this girl, pressed to his side, and throw her onto the bed. With a huge effort, he walked away and sat in his armchair, almost falling as he lowered himself. She followed and sat on his chair's arm, her legs resting on his.

"How did you find me, Max? How do you know so much about us? It is clever, and I think we could do much together, you and me. I escape from people who control family and work with you. I am clever too, I can be great use to you and the people you work with, like your UK cyber security council, are these the people you work with?"

Max was confused, he couldn't understand what was happening to him and he couldn't fight against it.

"You're a very beautiful and very intelligent woman, Daria, it would be very easy to love you," said Max, all senses of self-protection dispelled by the fentanyl.

She put her lips on his as her hand slowly, purposefully, slid up his thigh; Max was lost, breathless, stimulated beyond reason by the woman and by the drug.

"Then perhaps that is how it will be," murmured Daria into Max's ear. "We no more enemies, we are allies, we are lovers, and we fight together."

"Wouldn't that be wonderful, you come in from the cold, like a spy, and together we take on the world!" he said.

"How could it be so?"

"You could work with me, live with me, and we'd fight the trolls and hackers from my home," Max remembered what it was like to be an adolescent again; he felt youthful and irresponsible.

"Is a wonderful dream, wonderful but not possible, we two are not enough, who would help Max and Daria to take on world?"

"It isn't only me, you dafty," giggled Max, "it is the entire, brilliant company that is Onetelcall that is doing all the hard, clever work. It is Onetelcall, a grand Alliance of brilliance. We are on top of our game together, I can tell you."

He wanted to explain what he meant by 'Alliance', but his racing mental faculties couldn't quite cope with the complexity of any description.

"The Alliance is actually Onetelcall, is that how it is, Max? Is all snooping and prying on foreign farms done here by your company?"

"Of course, lovely girl, of course, all done here, all done by us, me and my colleagues, we don't need help, we ride alone like gunslingers in the wild west. Bang bang, you're dead." Max waved his two-finger pistol around the room, shooting imaginary baddies.

She could feel he was losing the ability to answer questions fully but tried to put the pieces of information together.

"You not cowboy, you modern man, thinker, do-er, lover, not shooter and ranch hand like old movie."

Max gazed at her, his feelings altering from dreamy make-believe to a surge of lust and want. He felt for her dress zip and began, slowly, to pull it down. Daria didn't attempt to stop him; she wriggled onto his knee, her hand now firmly where she wanted it to be.

"What about America, Max? Surely you have Onetelcall in America. They must fight with you, don't they?"

"Oh yeah," replied Max with uncharacteristic bombast, "there is always America, they're good too, you know, but all the action comes through us here, we are the champions… we are the champions of the world…"

She was losing him again; the zip was stationary, his libido visibly waning.

Another drink? Take him to bed? Change the subject to raunch and turn him on again? Daria was pondering her options when sirens screamed the presence of the emergency services in the car park below her window. She could hear shouts and radio conversations from the police cars beneath. She gathered that two men had been found, tied and beaten in one of the hotel rooms and guessed they would be Gary and Brian.

Daria took stock of her position. She believed that Onetelcall was the centre of the operations threatening her family and its networks. She understood there was an Alliance of some sort, and the Americans were involved. Destroy Onetelcall, that's what she had to do, destroy Onetelcall and its people. She made a quick call to Alex and fled via the back door to the car park. Duggie saw her get into her car and drive away. Worried, he ran to the hotel to find Max.

23

Angelo and Jesus were getting bored.

"This is fucking babysitting, it is not what we do," declared Angelo as he left the hotel room where Max was dozing happily, unharmed, in an armchair.

"Yeah, man," answered Jesus, "tell you what, we give it one more day and then we report back that we give this up and go back home for work we are better suited for."

"Agreed, man, agreed. Tell you what too, this Max guy has his own little dude trailing him around, makes me wonder if we ain't a duplication."

"Yeah, apart from jumpin' that big arsehole and handin' him over to the other guys in the ambulance get-up, we've not been able to do much real work. I'm bored, man, bored."

"Yeah, me too, and I miss the States; this fucking hotel is too fucking English for me, no broads, no burgers, no beer that I can drink, shithole man."

"Love the car though, bro, it's neat. I may get one like it when we're back; go to one of them Mecum auctions and pick up an awesome resto."

"Yeah, look man, before we quit, I have a feelin' we should trail the blond-haired babe; if she's just left the Max dude to wallow, you can bet she's up to something and I guess it is our job to cover her, I ain't getting on no plane with a job half done behind me."

"Agreed, man agreed, ain't no danger I can see for your man upstairs now the doll's gone, and his little dude can carry on with the babysitting for sure. My guess is that she's headin' back to that farmhouse, so, yeah, I guess that's where we should head off to, and I'm drivin' man, ok?"

Angelo threw the car keys in tacit agreement. Jesus fired up the Healy and it took the enthusiastically driven sports car just fifteen minutes to eat up the five minutes head start Daria had. They followed at a distance through the North Oxfordshire lanes and saw her turn off through a five-bar gated entrance and down to the drive of the now-familiar farmhouse. Jesus parked in the usual hiding place and clambered out from the old-fashioned, cramped driving position.

"My ass is tellin' me it don't want to sit no more, I'm thinkin' the Daria girl and the guy will be makin' plans, so I'm goin' for a spot of spying and see what I can hear."

"You talk like a jerk sometimes, man," grinned Angelo at his brother's mix of senses, "but it's a plan; I'll stay here and text an update to Art, promised we'd keep him posted all the way."

Jesus adjusted his sunglasses and, for a big man, made his way towards the farmhouse with the light-footed easy grace of a dancer.

Alex had heard Daria crunch the gravel drive to his back door and ran out to greet her. They hugged and, as luck would have it for Jesus, instead of going indoors, they made for the garden table and chairs. Eavesdropping made easy, thought Jesus.

"Drug worked, thank you, Alex," Daria was saying as Jesus began to listen, "and bastard Golby, he told me what I asked as I said he would."

"Did he give you any trouble?"

"He was, as you say, putty," she said, blushing slightly, "he was lust for me, and I played him like professional Marta Hari. He like Daria very much, very obviously."

"So how come you are here so early? I wasn't expecting you for hours yet, even tomorrow morning?"

"Two things Alex; the first is that I give too much drug, I think. He drank and soon he was excited and talk a lot, we get close, and he tell me answers to my questions, I say more about this in a minute, but then he get like idiot, he is sexy, then sleepy, he make less sense. I am thinking of new plan when police come to hotel, lots of police because I think they find Gary and Brian in room but I not understand what happened to them, anyway, I leave quick, very quick, bastard Golby asleep in chair, no more I can do."

"I see, are Gary and Brian, ok?"

"Not know, not wait to see, I think so though, didn't hear anything about dead bodies, just about two men. My guess is that whoever took them to room, made them talk about what they know, maybe they have torture or beating but not dead I think."

Jesus smiled to himself; it would have been a different story if he and Angelo had been the inquisitors.

"Whatever," said Alex, "it's good to have you back here safe and sound, my little niece, my plemyannitsa, tell me now, what did you find out, eh? Your plan of seduction and cross-questioning worked, did it? What's the story now? Are we going to war again with your new admirer?"

"You laugh at Daria? Well, I tell you Daria did better than good and bastard Golby, he fall for me, he want me," she shook her head and tossed her hair with mock vanity, "and he tell me what we much know. Now Alex, I know what we must do. I have plan and plan needs you and your bomb."

"Oh really, do you? Going bombing are we? Well first, let's hear your plan and you tell me just who or what we are going to blow up, where and why. Remember Daria, I'll support you all the way but I'm not getting killed or going to prison for you, so it had better be a good plan."

"You worry about Alex, always what you will do and what you not do. Daria think only of family and of business. She do whatever must be done for family good and take what risk must be taken. You owe me, you owe family, you do what I do. My plan will be good plan; we not die, we not get caught."

"Ok, ok, but while we're on the subject of what I won't do, I won't be responsible for bombing innocent people. Understand me well, Daria, I am not a killer and I want no part of killing people where they sit, no matter what the family thinks. The family owes me too, you know, we work together on even terms, and I won't be browbeaten into doing anything I can't do, even I have a conscience, you know."

"Huh."

"Don't get ratty, I've said what I have to say, now let's start work on your plan; give me the basics first."

Daria felt a familiar stab of cold malice at the full impact of Alex's unfamily-like faintheartedness. His willingness to act as a bomb man was commendable but his craven attitude to dying and killing was a cause of concern and regret. She feared he might let her down in a crisis of survival and regret because she might have to kill him if he turned traitor. With an edge of caution, she began to outline her crude but effective idea.

"Bastard Golby, he tell me that Onetelcall in UK is centre for vile spying into family business, he tell me that Onetelcall in America spies too but all is controlled by UK. He tell that there is some sort of Alliance but that Onetelcall is boss, everything that happens to family is because of his and his people in Olderbury.

"You sure that's correct? Seems to me that all the activity is a more global effort than anything Onetelcall could manage on its own."

"Maybe it is, maybe bastard Golby not tell me all, too much drug I think, but I know this, Alexandru, we start revenge, we start protecting family business, we start all this at Onetelcall, we bomb the whole company into nothing, they stop us, we stop them. And Ok, we do this at night, so all their spying computers and equipment gets blown up but no people in office at time of bomb, does that satisfy you?"

"Yeah, that fits with me splendidly, and it is a starting point. I agree, even if the international activity isn't all down to Onetelcall, we sure as hell will slow them down and give them something to think about. Another thing, Daria, we had better do whatever your plan says we should do pretty quickly. The news from Chisinau is that the entire operation is on stop because it is being constantly monitored; they want us, you, to act and act quickly."

"Then we do it tonight, Alex. Tonight, in Olderbury, there will be big fireworks!"

Jesus had heard enough. He sprinted back to the car and booted the big Healy all the way back to The Royal George, where he reported his news to Angelo who, in turn, sent an intelligence-rich missive to Art.

"Should we break cover and tell the Max dude do you think, bro?" asked Jesus.

"No, our job is always the same, we watch, we act, we hit who we are told to hit and protect who we are told to protect because we are the best at doing what we do; that's all there is, we don't put our noses into places they shouldn't oughta be put. Agree?"

"Agreed. But got our work cut out, man, those two crazies have real bomb power, and even you and me can't beat up a pack of plastic."

"Yeah, mad Max is our orders, and he is who we have to look out for, and we gotta be smart, this is a different now, it ain't just protection or popping off a bad man, this is saving a guy from an explosion, maybe we stop the crazies, maybe we just save Max and anyone else at the time, we'll see what rolls."

"Agreed, man, we better split right now and get to mad Max's pad; we left him alone with his little tail for too long."

"I got an idea, Jesus, how about we separate? I know it ain't our usual m.o. but this time we got lots to look after. It ain't our brief to protect no buildings and all that, but we need to know what the crazies are doing if we are going to make sure our man stays living. I'll drop you off at Onetelcall and go on to his pad; we keep in touch on our cell phones, don't matter if they are bust by a listener now; we just do our jobs, yeah?"

"Agreed, man agreed. I'm cool with that, just go by way of the store so I can get some coffee, yeah?

"Yeah, me too man."

It was twilight when the Healy pulled into a layby fifty yards from Onetelcall's main entrance.

"Ok, Jesus, this is where it's all going to go down, fuck knows what's going to happen but you gotta watch it man, and keep our dude away from any big bangs or people with guns, yeah?"

"Agreed, man," replied Jesus, "I'm going to take a position over there," he pointed to a dark area inside the car park and with a view of the building's front entrance, car park and delivery doorways.

"Cool," commented Angelo, "no way to get to your back and you have plenty of viewing angle, good spot. See ya, man, stay safe and keep in touch when it gets interesting, agreed?"

"Agreed man."

Jesus smiled to himself as the sound of the Healy faded into the distance, 'gotta get one of those beauts', he thought to himself, not for the first time since they had hired the old sports car. He settled down on a level spot, Onetelcall's well-tended shrubbery masking his position. He sat back, warmed by a coffee, his mind wandering. 'That Max dude sure got some balls', he mused, 'he coulda run but he's hangin' in there, him and his little compadre'. Jesus was always impressed by those he referred to as 'los duendes' when they displayed valour and a dogged refusal to be beaten. He could cope with protecting people like Max; he resented the times gone by when he and Angelo had risked their lives to shield the wasters and punks who proliferated in the drug business. Now he was happy safeguarding Jimmy, his family and their close associates and only rarely did he and Angelo sell their skills to qualified outsiders, and then only for an extortionately high price.

Years of experience had taught Jesus how to relax before any confrontation, and he was in a meditative state between sleep and awake when he heard an engine. Alert in an instant, he instinctively crouched a little lower as he saw a car he'd seen in Alex's farmyard turn slowly into the Onetelcall car park. 'Idiots', he thought, 'if you don't want to be noticed, don't drive around with no lights on'.

Two figures emerged, and Jesus watched as Daria and Alex opened the boot of their car and extracted some large bags. From the back seat, Alex pulled out more bags and, by the light of a focused torch, began to unpack. Through his night-vision binoculars, Jesus saw Alex unwrap what he knew to be Orica wireless detonators and begin the task of inserting them gently into wrapped cartons of explosives. Jesus was a sturdy, muscular man but he could move with a stealthy grace. He manoeuvred himself to within earshot of the two bombers.

"You sure we have enough for job, it is a big building?"

"Relax, Daria, we have enough material here to take out most of the town; this will be a pile of rubble when I've finished."

"You sure we can destroy building without going inside?"

"Daria, for Christ's sake, we've been through this a dozen times. Trust me, the building will be obliterated, and you will be able to tell your family that you have succeeded without killing anyone."

"It is good, Alex, that we destroy the Onetelcall home of bastards, but I think I kill bastard Golby anyway, perhaps not tonight in explosion, but soon, you see, soon."

"You're single-minded Daria, I'll give you that, but, just for now, let's concentrate on the job at hand, shall we?"

Alex straightened himself from his stooping position and, Jesus could see, mentally planned his next steps.

"We can't risk setting off their alarms, and this place is impenetrable when all its alarms are active," said Alex surveying the building he already knew in detail from plans he had acquired from his cash-hungry contact in the council planning office, "but we can get to the roof where I believe there are pressure pads near obvious points of access but not near the vents and flues."

He looked at Daria, whose eyes were luminous, shimmering with excitement. This would be her job as she could climb vertical walls with minimum foothold, a technique she had acquired as a girl, climbing in the Cornesti hills accompanied and tutored by a cat-burglar occasionally employed by Familie Odin.

Alex and Daria prepared to plant their explosives. Alex arranged the packs, all fitted with as-yet unarmed radio detonators along an unlit back wall while Daria checked her powerful vacuum suction pads and lightweight rope, ready for her ascent.

Jesus silently retreated to his original position from where he could see most of the front and car-park side of the building and the side wall, which he assumed would be where Daria would climb. He was peering through his night-sight glasses at the roof for a visual reconnoitre of her most feasible route when he heard another vehicle approaching. Alex and Daria heard it too. They swiftly hid the climbing gear but had no time to move the packs of explosives. Jesus saw them scurry behind a salt bunker just before headlights swept into the car park. Jesus saw two men in the car; one was mad Max and the other, the driver, his constant companion and tail. He saw Max point at Alex's car. He saw the smaller man nod. He knew this was the beginning of an unstoppable event that could end badly.

24

Duggie, running quickly after seeing Daria drive away, had got to Max just minutes after Jesus and Angelo had left the hotel room. At first, Max hadn't responded to Duggie shaking his shoulder but did come round after Duggie ventured a light slap. Max's drugged, sleepy eyes opened, and he grinned stupidly at his friend.

"I think she slipped me a micky, mate," he murmured.

Duggie grinned like a schoolboy, "Oh yeah, what did you slip her then, eh?"

Eventually, Duggie got Max to stand up and walk unsteadily around the room.

"We ought to fuck off Max," advised Duggie, "there's feds all over the fucking place, something's gone down in one of the other rooms, so we should make ourselves scarce before we get caught up in whatever's happening."

Max concentrated on staying upright and putting one foot in front of the other. With Duggie steering him by the elbow, the two men made it out of the hotel and to Duggie's car without hindrance. In the fresh air, Max's memory began to work overtime.

"I reckon the feds have found those two blokes, you know, Gary and Brian, that's what all this fuss is about," he said with increasing clarity of mind.

"So, what happened with the girl in her hotel room then, big man?"

"You've got a seedy mind you have Duggie, but I'll tell you this, you're not far wrong, she's one tricky lady that Daria and if she were anyone else, I'd be after her like the proverbial. Trouble is, she's a fucking loony, Dug, fucking loony, I tell you. She only fucking drugged me, draping her legs all over me and sending the old todge into diamond-cutter territory. I fell for it, Duggie, I fucking fell for it. If I could have worked out which way was up, I'd have had her on the spot, except I wouldn't though, would I? I mean, it was all just a game to her, just a trap, just a way of beating me and getting any info she could out of me."

"Did she get anything Max, I mean, what did you tell her?"

"I dunno, Dug, that's the truth. I was so out of it, I just don't know. But I do know this, chap, I do know we should allow for me mouthing off too much, telling her too much, I don't know, but too much anyway, perhaps about what we've found out about her goddam Familie Odin and the Chisinau operation, perhaps about the Alliance. I don't know, but it's fair to assume the worst isn't it."

Duggie agreed as he parked outside Max's flat. "Come on, mate, I'll make you some of your coffee."

While Duggie fought with Max's complex coffee maker, Max called Art to warn him that he may have been a major leaker of information to Daria the seductress.

"It's a bit early for all this, Max," moaned Art, still in bed, "and to be honest, Max. I don't give a damn right now because you've got bigger problems. I think you're about to be bombed."

"What the…"

"Yeah, Max, I've had a word from the Alliance's ears on Chisinau and, could be wrong, of course, but it looks like Alex is helping Daria with some bomb-making gear, plastic explosive from what we gather. Anyway, it seems he sent a report, an update, saying Daria was planning on bombing Onetelcall and everyone in it."

"Oh Christ, Art, I want to say that she wouldn't do that but after my last encounter with her, I know that she would; she's completely off her rocker, you know."

"Yeah, that's for sure, but it seems like your man Alex isn't quite crazy. He's told the family in Moldova that he'll help her, but he won't have any part in any killing. Now, we are pretty sure that he has killed in the past, so quite why he is so moral about it now, we don't understand, nor are we sure how you can bomb a building without risking death, but there you go."

"Best guess is that they'll try to take out the offices and all the equipment at night then, that way they will stop us from crippling their black operations for their drugs and their state-sponsored trolling and, at night, the offices will be empty, or emptier anyway. Thing is, we do have some people monitoring traffic through the night; I think I ought to tell them right now, the best I can do is ensure no one is in the building tonight because it will be tonight, won't it, Art?"

"Yeah, Max, it'll be tonight, that's for sure. Stay away, no heroics, stay away."

"Bye Art."

"OK, Duggie, I have to tell you, this is getting deadly again, chap, and if you want out, I'd totally understand. In fact, I'm thinking of getting the hell away from here myself. We are fighting nutters, that Daria wants us dead, no two ways, mate, she's a killer, and she's got us, me for sure, in her sights."

"Look, Max," answered Duggie with unusual earnestness, "it isn't like you saved my life or anything, but you have given me a life, a life I can be proud of for the first time ever. If I quit now, I might just as well be nobby again, no mates, no self-respect, no nothing. And you, look at you, I leave you on your own for five minutes and you get yourself drugged up by a deranged seductress. I mean."

Max smiled at his friend with a shame-faced expression which, Duggie could see, was an unaccustomed expression for him.

"You might not believe this Dug, old boy, but sometimes it is you who gives me strength, you're right, of course, neither of us can run away now," he paused, looking pensive and then added, "so come on Duggie boy let's get to it, you be Flash, I'll be Gordon."

"But we haven't even got twenty-four hours to save the world," answered Duggie wryly.

Max called his office and talked to his designated safety officer, Judith Grey.

"It's Judith, that you Max? And if you hey Jude me, you can fuck straight off."

"Hey Jude," answered Max, "for once, we have to have a serious conversation, I'm afraid."

"Really? That'll be a first then, don't tell me you're taking safety seriously at last?"

"I always take you seriously Judith, after all, it was you who alerted me to the danger of staplers."

"Like I said, fuck straight off, Max."

"Judith, this is serious, really and what I'm about to tell you isn't a joke, far from it. You know we've been involved in an initiative to track hackers and trolls, don't you?"

"How could I not? It is the only thing anyone talks about around here."

"We've upset some very nasty people, and I have good reason to believe they may try to plant a bomb in our offices tonight."

"Crikey Max, are you for real?"

"Deadly, and I mean that. Here's what I want you to do…" Max explained his plan in detail and Judith, now every inch the professional asked the right questions and left Max assured that his wishes would be executed precisely.

"What about the police?"

"I know you are supposed to inform the authorities of anything and everything you feel they should know, but in this case, I don't want them involved. I would explain but it would take too long. Can you please trust me on this?"

"You know it, Max."

"Hey, boss, Said Duggie as Max hung up, "I've been doing some of that what you call thinking, and I reckon there's no way in the creation of bollocks that the loonies are loony enough to try to break into the building. I mean, it's alarmed to high heavens and they won't be able to find a way around our systems, that's a fact innit. So, what are they going to do at night eh? They blow the baseline, won't they? They'll put explosives all around the base of the building and blow its foundations out, so it crumbles down like them controlled explosions on tower blocks and that."

"That's good thinking, Duggie; it makes a lot of sense. Unless they've got someone on the inside, which is possible, they'll never get inside, will they?" Max looked pensive again.

"Tell you what though, if it were me, I'd want to blow the insides too, just to be sure I'd take all the kit out, stop all the work dead for a long, long time. Would I, could I get some explosive in from the roof, I wonder?"

"Hmmm, only if you could get to the roof without triggering an alarm. All the windows are wired too, you know, and you'd have to be fucking spiderman to get on the roof without tripping something, somewhere. Even so…" He called Judith again to add another item to his list of instructions.

"Up to you Dug," he continued. "Stay here if you like or pop back home, but I'm going to get a bit of sleep before tonight, still feeling the after-effects of that bloody drug Daria gave me, and I reckon we'll need our wits around us when the action starts."

"Nah, I'll stay if that's ok. I'm going to raid your 'fridge and kick that fucking coffee machine around a bit more. You nod off and I'll wake you, if I need to, when it starts to get dark."

It was just before seven in the evening when Max woke Duggie, who had snoozed on his sofa.

"What do you reckon, James Bond or what?" Max was dressed in a black roll-neck, black jeans and black trainers.

"You'll get nicked by the thought police for appropriation," laughed Duggie, "but I suppose you've dressed right for the occasion. I'm treating it as a come-as-you-are party, obviously,"

"You look lovely Dug, just as long as you are dressed with your gun handy, we'll be fine."

Duggie patted what had become his gun pocket reassuringly. He took his pistol out and checked it over, making sure the clip was still full of bullets, although why it shouldn't be, he didn't quite know.

"What else do you need, guv?"

"All the phones, Duggie, we need a pair dedicated to talk and text between you and me, and the others will be used, one for other outside calls and the rest for monitoring cameras; Jude will have sent the links to me by now. That old Samsung, we'll keep for monitoring the Alliance traffic, I think, you never know what they might pick up, and Art has promised to relay it all over an onion messenger to a secure burner phone if I give him the number."

"What about you? Are you going to carry anything to protect yourself with?"

Max chuckled and looked a little embarrassed as he pulled a small multi-purpose penknife from his pocket.

"Oh great," said Duggie grinning widely, "if we need to extract a boy scout from a girl guide, it's good to know you've got the right tool."

"Bollocks."

"OK then 007, what's the game plan for tonight then? I suppose you've got a plan like you always have?"

"As it happens Douglas, I have, but I must say it's a bit shaky, and it depends on people doing what I expect them to do, so it doesn't come with any guarantees."

Max poured another two coffees and ran through his thoughts, asking Duggie for any comments and suggestions as he went. At the end of the conversation, Duggie said, "Sounds great, Max, very clever but have you got plans B, C and D up your sleeve? I mean, if everything goes as you predict, then you've got it right, but the likelihood is that the loonies won't act in any predictable way, and the plan goes to shit, yeah?"

"Undooobitably, my little critical pal, and we may go to shit with it, but in the absence of anything better, let's take our chances with what we've got and make it up as it goes along if the best-laid plans gang awry."

Duggie had parked a little way away from the Onetelcall building, and the two of them waited until the car, headlights off, carrying Alex and Daria, turned into the office's car park.

"Ah-ha," said Max with mock joy, "the first part of the plan goes like clockwork; they are here as predicted."

"Right on, Nostradamus."

"Let's wait for, what, ten minutes? Then we'll drive in, make a point of noticing their car and then drive out again, that'll unnerve them, I'll leap out when we are out of sight again. Jude will have sent me a code for the garden door, and I'll slip in through there. It's right at the other side from them, they won't spot me. You know what to do after that?"

"Roger that, Roger."

Max glanced at Duggie who, for reasons Max couldn't understand, seemed happier, funnier, sharper and more alive than he'd ever seen him. Adrenaline or just the joy of self-realisation, he wondered.

"Ok, go for plan item number two, Duggie, the drive-in and out."

Duggie's full-beam headlights quickly illuminated the parked car and the row of packages stacked against the rear wall. They didn't shine on Jesus, nor had Duggie's mirrors alerted them to the presence of a Healy, under some trees, some hundred yards behind where they had been parked.

It wasn't only Daria and Alex who were bemused by the in-and-out car ploy. Jesus observed with a little confusion but guessed it was a ruse of some sort. If so, he approved.

Sitting snugly in his shaped leather seat, Angelo watched Duggie's Ford go into the car park, come out again, pause in a semi-concealed spot and then return to its parking place. Angelo, too, guessed the purpose of this move. 'Bet Jesus likes that', he thought.

After slipping out of the car unnoticed, Max's first task, once inside through the garden door as planned, was to check that the building was, indeed, empty. Although only the obligatory emergency lights were shining, Max took care to stay in the dark, away from any windows and careful of casting any moving shadows. Satisfied that he was alone, he sprinted up to the inspection gangway in the roof and checked all the security panels; again, Judith had done her job well. Max marvelled at what guile she must have used to explain her actions. Then, he ran down to the plant room and turned all the boilers up to full heat, ensuring that their exhaust gasses would be at maximum temperature.

Finally, he went to a small exit door behind the plant room and disarmed its alarm. Having a choice of two fast exists somehow made sense. With his initial task list completed, Max's energy surge diminished and was replaced by growing anxiety and apprehension. Even though Daria's target was the building and not him this time, he couldn't help but feel an irrepressible rush of mortality. His stomach tightened and his nerves jarred. Confident, without certainty, that the building was secure against any entry by Daria and Alex, he followed his plan and went outside through the same door by which he had entered. He left it unlocked and just latched for fast use.

He made his way to the tall perimeter hedge on the far side of the building from the car park and Alex and Daria's centre of activity. Here he sent a text to Duggie, confirming that the checks and preparations had all been made. Duggie started the car and, as quietly as possible, drove it into the splay of Onetelcall's entrance road and parked across it. No vehicles could leave the building now.

Angelo had been trying to choose between joining Jesus and staying outside, ready to pounce on any stray crazies and to keep an eye on Max's little friend too. When Duggie blocked the entrance road, Angelo chose to stay outside. There was a flashpoint in the making, he thought.

Dara and Alex heard the sound of a car start but took no notice; it was too far distant to be of immediate concern. Alex did a final visual sweep of the area. He didn't see Jesus, he didn't see Max, he couldn't see Duggie or his car and, to Alex's sharp eyes, everything looked quiet. He knew that their arrival and subsequent activities would be recorded on Onetelcall's security cameras but didn't care. If the recordings were held locally, they would soon be vapourised. If they were set to a remote location then, as there had been no reaction to their presence, he deduced he and Daria would be long gone by the time the building became Olderbury's biggest-ever bonfire.

"Ok, girl, time to get climbing and don't forget what I've told you, keep off the glass and away from the windows, they will be live, and any tremor will make them sound off. When you get to the top, walk around the perimeter ring beam wall, the bit that stands proud at the edge, there are no alarms there. And remember, too, it is imperative that the inside bombs blow before the outside; that way, the building will fall in, implode as it explodes, if you see what I mean."

"Ok, got that."

"Sure you know which flues and vents?"

"Of course, and how to get to them, yes, I know."

"Keep your phone and ping me if you have any problems,

ok?"

"Ok, see you, Alex."

Daria activated the suction pad vacuum and set off on her climb, her backpack filled with explosive parcels.

25

Max's initial instinct on hearing about a possible bomb attack on his building was to try to stop it and save the building and all its equipment. Art had counselled against this, pointing out the evident dangers and likelihood of failure. Against his better judgement, Max had acceded. In his list of actions for Judith, he had insisted that all information held on all their machines be copied onto physical, transportable media and taken away from the office. He had eschewed using any electronic transfer for security reasons. He had also asked Judith to instruct the techs to remove all the most vital equipment and take it away, as most of the pieces were small and portable. By the time the offices were evacuated for an emergency drill, most of the remaining equipment was possibly the most expensive but the least pivotal.

Jesus was watching as Daria prepared for her ascent. He could see her heavy backpack, filled with explosives. He sent a text to Angelo. Angelo replied, saying 'stay still'.

Slowly and carefully, she began to climb, using what tiny abutments in the steel cladding she could find for footholds. Her high vacuum suction pads, with turn grip for suction, flip lever to release, were easy, fast and secure. As her confidence grew, so did her rate of climb, and within ten minutes of exertion, she was at the top, perched, as instructed, on the wide ring beam ledge. She looked around, over the lights of Olderbury, down to the car park and saw the entrance driveway was blocked by a stationary car. For once, her senses let her down, and she imagined a courting couple rather than a threat to her mission. She looked for Alex but couldn't see him as he had begun his journey around the base of the building, planting packages of explosives, at measured distances. She decided to get into the most central flues and work her way, radially outwards, using only strengthening steel protrusions as her walkway, which as Alex had told her, would not be alarmed or conceal pressure pads.

She reached the central fitment and found it to be a large flue with four separate exhausts in it, and it was burning hot, almost too hot to approach. Surely the explosive would ignite the moment it was subjected to such direct heat? She sent an urgent text to Alex, who replied immediately, advising her to leave the hottest pipes alone and go for the smaller, cooler vents.

Daria walked back a few feet to a cooler area and arranged the packages, initially meant for the exhausts, in a circle around the large flue. Better this than no bomb at all at this central location, she reasoned to herself. Gradually and cautiously, she approached each vent, posted the especially slim packages through the slats and lowered them by their attached string, until they reached a resting place. She checked each package, making sure the detonator was firm and its wi-fi beacon free and open to the airwaves.

With four bombs placed on the roof around the central flue and eight other packages lowered into the building through the vents, Daria delivered twelve bombs in all. She had no idea what this meant in terms of explosive force, but Alex had assured her the bang would be biblical.

She texted 'done' to Alex. He replied, 'come down, I'm halfway'.

As it had taken Alex all the time she had spent posting her bombs to get halfway around the base of the building, she need not hurry to leave the roof and start her improvised abseil back to the ground.

Alex was being punctilious in placing his bombs. He loved explosives, and although he had insisted that nobody should die in this attack, he relished their power to deliver destruction and desolation. His bombs were larger than Daria's, each containing two sticks of EPX-2, both just over 500mm long and about 40mm square. He had a dozen of them, enough to blow the building to pieces. "Better be some way away when this lot blows," he said to himself as he delicately placed charge number six in a carefully chosen internal corner. Like Daria, he checked each bomb as he placed it, ensuring that the wi-fi was free and clear and the detonator well-placed.

He texted Daria again, 'fast, need to get away'.

He hit the send button and as he turned to pick up his bags, he saw Duggie, only briefly but enough to know he wasn't alone. Duggie had been following Alex around the building, pulling out the detonators Alex had so carefully checked. Max had suggested they should try to save the building and following Alex had been Duggie's idea, despite Max protesting that it was too dangerous.

"Nobody has ever noticed me before," said Duggie by way of justification of his plan, "no reason to think that'll change tonight."

Alex turned forward and, bags in hand set off on his route around the building. Not suspecting he'd been seen, Duggie followed at his estimated safe distance. Squatting down and rubbing his shoulder along the wall, Duggie made himself as small as possible, but his prowling position made him slower to react. When Alex sprang out at him from around a corner, he couldn't defend himself and Alex's first blow sent him falling backwards, head against the wall, legs sprawling in front of him. Alex moved in for a second blow, and Duggie yelped in pain as a furious fist dislocated his jaw. He shielded his eyes with his arm in a feeble attempt to repel another fist strike. It didn't come. No follow-up punch, no more excruciating pain, just a gasp of breath and the heavy thud of a sizeable body hitting the ground.

Duggie moved his arm and opened his eyes, his jaw feeling like someone had tied an anvil to his cheeks. He saw Alex, inert on the ground and the shadow of a large man receding into the darkness, holding a phone to his ear. In seconds, Max was by his friend's side, tending to him and using his handkerchief as a makeshift face sling. Suddenly, he saw Alex come to brandishing a remote control.

"I press this button, the building disappears," he growled.

"You press that button, we all disappear, and Daria is still on the roof."

Alex shook his head, trying to clear his mind after the almighty whack Jesus had delivered to knock him out.

"Not down yet eh? Well, fuck her. Get that tosser on his feet, do what I say if you want to live, personally, I'm beyond caring if I push this button or not."

Max looked at Alex and believed him.

"Come on, old mate, let's do what the nice man asks, shall we?" He helped a groggy Duggie to his feet.

"Ok, walk away, you two, to the car park and fast, yeah?"

Max turned, planning to attempt a counter-attack but saw Alex had added a small handgun to his remote control.

"Either I blow you up, or I shoot you. Do you have a preference?"

"We'll walk," said Max.

Max and Duggie made slow progress and Alex was getting impatient. As they neared the car park, Alex made a break and ran to his car.

Daria watched furiously from the roof. "What's going on?" she yelled.

Alex looked up at her perched on the edge of the beam and fired a shot at her. She screamed and fell backwards out of sight. Alex stumbled into his car, the tyres screeching with wheelspin as he raced away, only to slam headlong into Duggie's roadblock around the corner from the car park. He clambered out, blood streaming from his forehead and fired two shots in the general direction of where Max and Duggie would have been had they been chasing him. Alex turned and half ran, half staggered past the crashed cars, towards the main road.

For the second time that evening, Jesus's favoured gloved upper cut laid Alex out, unconscious on the road. As he hit the ground, his hand compressed over his remote control's red button and the fires of hell appeared in Olderbury. High up on the roof, the after-thought circle of explosives that Daria had laid around the central flue blew with unimaginable ferocity; it destroyed the roof structure instantly, and Daria, already in agony with a bullet in her shoulder, fell into a flaming Hades of her own creation.

Max and Duggie were blown across the car park for some twenty feet. Max's all-black clothing and skin underneath ripped and tore as he skidded along the tarmac with the force of the blast. Duggie, already in considerable pain, passed out as his head crashed against the ground.

Jesus had been running away from the site entrance after laying Alex low and was level with the driveway's defining wall when the bombs exploded. Partly shielded from the force, he was blown to the ground and would have only sustained mild bruising had the wall not disintegrated in the blast, throwing bricks and mortar into the air, some of which landed on his prone body. A large half-brick struck the back of his head, and Jesus slumped back, unconscious and bleeding.

Angelo, who had taken station across the road from the main entrance after Duggie had moved his car, had been watching Daria on the roof, saw her shot, and then, seconds later, the blinding flare of the explosive eruption on the roof. He caught the percussive violence of the blast a nano-second later and, although he was some metres away, felt himself propelled backwards into the roadside bushes. The dense shrubs acted as a catch fence and halted him, head-buzzing, aching everywhere but essentially uninjured.

Max was sitting up, confused and in pain, making an inventory of his body, when the first of the emergency services arrived and set about moving Duggie's car to gain access to the burning building. The police led the charge, quickly followed by a succession of more police cars and, next, the Olderbury fire service's two tenders and its emergency rescue vehicle, followed only minutes later by the first of the ambulances.

Max watched in detached bemusement as the fire officers got to work in an impressive display of coordinated efficiency. Hoses were unfurled, ladders deployed, hydrants tapped, and the firefighting began in earnest.

The Onetelcall building was like a volcano, with flames erupting from its roof and molten debris flowing down its walls. Max gazed, still dazed, expecting to see destruction and devastation, but Duggie had done a good job, and only two of Alex's base bombs detonated. Where they had exploded, they had obliterated a large corner of the building where the gym, kitchens, stores, toilets, showers and workshops had once been. The rest of the building still stood; only the roof and second-floor areas were ablaze.

Max's attention was diverted by two angelically blue eyes looking at him from over a face mask.

"I'm just going to give you something for the pain if that's alright?"

His mind wanted to do the small prick joke, but he couldn't make his body respond. He felt the needle and knew no more. He didn't see Angelo carrying his brother to their car. The immaculate Healy had a side window blown out but was driveable. He didn't see Jesus falling back into the passenger seat, conscious again and cursing loudly when Angelo stamped on the throttle and sped away.

26

Max had been transferred to Royal United City hospital, where the tissue viability team had created a regime for his badly scored skin and multiple severe abrasions. He hadn't broken any bones, but muscles, ligaments and tendons, all over his body had been ripped; he was in less pain, and the Tramadol kept it that way.

"It must be my week for blue eyes," he said as he greeted Detective Sergeant Amanda Cotter.

"Mr Golby," said Amanda, pulling a straight-backed vinyl chair to Max's bedside, "I am DS Cotter from Olderbury police station, and I am here to ask you some questions about what's been happening that could end with the bombing of the Onetelcall building."

"I remember you very well," said Max, "you were part of the investigation into my friend Jo Hadge's attack all that time ago. You were very kind to her, I remember. You were a WPC then, weren't you? DS now, eh? Doing well, that's just great; I'm sure you more than deserve it."

Amanda flushed slightly with delight. Even in the 21st century, the police force was not much given to complimenting its female officers and, outside the force, most people treated her with contempt if they were villains or with disdain and sarcasm if they were the usual brand of misogynist she so often met.

"I remember you too sir, and thank you, yes, I've been promoted and, actually, your friend Jo was very kind to me too. She wrote a letter of approval about me to the Chief Constable, and that was, I think, the beginning of me getting noticed."

Suffused with opiate-fed warmth and bonhomie, Max wanted to flirt with his visitor; she made his eyes happy and his mind joyful, but Amanda's professional demeanour deterred him, for now. Instead, he said,

"I've had very little news since that night. It was three days ago now but feels very distant and still a bit confused; what's been happening?"

"Well, I'm sure you know that most of the Onetelcall building was saved, the roof has gone, and two major sections of the structure are damaged beyond repair. The bomb guys say that if all the bombs had been planted and detonated, not only would that building have gone, but most of the entire trading estate and half the town would have been blown to bits by massive pressure waves."

"I'd heard it could have been a lot worse; that's down to Duggie, you know, he was a bloody hero, that chap."

"Yes, that's spot on, he was. He's doing fine, sir, as I'm sure you know. He's just down the corridor in the orthopaedic ward. His jaw is all wired up and he's got an arm in plaster but he's ok."

"Yeah, I know, I get regular reports on his progress, and if I can move without all my scratches opening up again, I'm off down to see him later or tomorrow anyway."

"Very good, sir…"

"It's Max, please, just call me Max, 'sir' was my granddad."

"Ok, Max, and I think you've got a bit more than just scratches under all that dressing. Are you doing ok?"

"Yes, ma'am, and I'm fine for answering some questions if that's what you mean?"

"I think perhaps Amanda rather than ma'am. I hope I don't look that matronly, even here in hospital."

"You look wonderful to me, Amanda, so shoot with your enquiries."

Amanda Cotter flushed for the second time. Usually blush-proof, she wondered why she was more susceptible to gentle flattery from this man.

"I don't know where to start. We are still piecing things

together, you know. Actually, between you and me, it's all a bit hellish. We have the bomb squad, an anti-terrorist unit, the drug unit, some Foreign Office spooks, an Interpol guy, and heaven knows who else, climbing over this case, all claiming authority and fighting each other like school kids."

Max smiled sympathetically, "Then we must make sure it is you who gets the inside track and all the glory, eh? I may well be too ill to talk to anyone else."

Amanda smiled her appreciation.

"What do you know, Amanda?"

"Well, we know, or at least we think we know, that there were two bombers, a man and a woman. The body of a woman was recovered from inside the building, when I say body, I mean burnt, charred bits of body which we are fairly sure was a woman, but the ghouls are still working on it."

"It was a woman," confirmed Max, "her name was Daria something. I can't remember if I ever knew her surname. She was Moldovan, and part of a powerful drugs and digital terrorism mob called Familie Odin."

"Thank you, we'll come back to that. What do you know about the man? He was found next to your mate Duggie; someone had hit him hard, he had concussion and was in a bit of state, on the point of losing it altogether, I think."

"Look, Amanda, I've got an idea which I think will help you. Why don't I write the whole sorry tale down, from when it all first started to the bombing three nights ago? Then you can read it and I'll answer any questions you have after that?"

"That would be wonderful. I was going to ask you for a simple statement, but I guess the circumstances are too complex for that, so if you can put it all down on paper, I'd really be grateful, especially if I get it first and no one else sees it."

Max grinned conspiratorially, "For your eyes only, Amanda."

"Oh, yuck."

"Sorry, look, it'll take me some time and I can guess you are in a rush. How about if I have it ready for you by the morning?"

"You sure you can do it that fast? I mean, are you feeling strong enough?"

"Yeah, I'm ok for a little light typing duty, must find a laptop from somewhere though, if I write it by hand, you'll never read it."

"Leave that to me, Max, I'll be back in no time with a machine for you. I'll nip to that discount shop and get a good cheapie for you."

"Thanks, Amanda, can you get me a charger for my phone too?"

Plugged in at last and charging from flat, Max could check his phone messages; there were many of them.

"I told you to stay safe! You're a bloody marvel. Jo sends her love. See you very soon, coming home next week. Dan."

"Alliance in full action now, factories and farms being blocked and closed all over the place. What you've done, Max, is having a worldwide effect. Get well soon, mate. Dan."

"Buy me another of those pub lunches, man? All cool here. Glad you ain't dead. Yet. Art."

"Our guys, you know who, are back home safe and sound. Speak well of you. That don't happen often. Art."

"You don't know us. We are always on your side. You know how to get us. Rent us a Healy if you need us."

"For once, I'm proud. If I can find a way, I'll see you soon. Good work Max. Brilliant and brave. Spray."

"Looks like my clients are turning colour, black to white. More when you are fit again. Interesting times. Up for more? Art."

"We think we owe you our lives. Thank you, Max. See you soon? Love Sue and Indira."

"Charger ok? Laptop ok? Dinner when you are out ok? Amanda x."

Max felt a frisson of pride and pleasure and excited anticipation of what he hoped would soon be a new, special relationship with DS Cotter.

With his new bargain laptop, he started writing his report of everything that had happened since Dan first initiated the Alliance and its investigations. He realised that even though Daria was dead and Alex in custody and very possibly a little unhinged, it wasn't all over. In some ways, it could never all be over, there would always be digital wrongdoers and online turpitude, and now Onetelcall had been internationally recognised as a white hat battler, there would always be danger and threats from the many sectors of illegality such as trolls, hackers, terrorists, pirates, pressure groups, even governments.

Had he missed a trick? Could he have arranged to disappear in the conflagration? Could he have been declared dead and not have to worry ever again? Writing more, thinking more deeply, Max knew he could never run away and hide, he'd joined a crusade from which there would be, could be, no resignation, no quitting.

"Wotcha, Mr Bond, how are they dangling?"

Max's thoughts were interrupted by a wheelchair being pushed into his sideward and Duggie's friendly, light-hearted voice bringing a welcome respite from his musings.

"Christ Dug, you look bloody awful."

"You too."

The two friends, brothers in arms now, shared a relaxed, celebratory laugh.

"Still alive then," observed Max.

"Fucking miracle that is," replied Duggie happily.

The nurse who had wheeled Duggie into Max's room

reappeared with a jug of hot coffee and two cups.

"Here you go, boys, keep you going while you swap war stories, and, Mr Duggie Miller, hero and action man, here's your straw."

After two hours of what-ifs, should haves, shouldn't haves and bloody hells, the conversation turned to the future. Max's solemnity returned.

"We've sort of won this one so far, mate, but the war isn't over. There will be more Darias, more Alexes, and they'll still be gunning for us."

"Yeah, I know that I do. But tell you something, I'm here to fight again now. You and me, Max, we've got no choice anymore." He leaned back in his wheelchair, his fingers playing over the wires clamping his jaw bones together. "Look, Max, you know a bit about me. Come from nothing, never done anything useful in my life. Just a no-one. Until now. Now I feel alive. I look in the mirror and I see someone I'm happy to be, for once, not some worthless loser who nobody cares about. Know what I mean Max? It's a bit of self-respect for once, a feeling of self-worth that I've never had. God knows, I'm not brave or anything like it. I was shitting conkers following that Alex around, pulling out those detonators. But I did it, for fuck's sake, I did it. Me, on my own. Might not be much to you, but to me, it's like I'm born again, born to be a something, a somebody, not a faceless, useless waster. Tell you something else too, if I get bumped off tomorrow or next week or next year because I've fought for something worth fighting for, then I'll be fucking happy. Better than dying being a nothing, a corpse with no previous, a life that didn't touch the surface, didn't make a ripple."

Max felt emotional, perhaps fuelled by the painkiller, perhaps because Duggie had touched a nerve and found something he could relate to but had ignored in himself for too long.

"You're too hard on yourself, Duggie," he replied, "you know good from bad, right from wrong and you choose to stand up for it. Brave or not, it doesn't matter. What matters is the strength, the resolve, and the determination to be the best you can be. To go to bed at night and take stock, to ask yourself if you did your best, if you hurt anyone, harmed anyone or did something you shouldn't have done. If you can go to sleep with a clear conscience, you're more of a man than most. Christ Duggie, I know what you did, you know what I did, we are neither of us saints and have a lot to regret in our lives, but what you just said is right, and I'm glad you said it."

"There you go then boss, what's the plan now then, eh? I take it you've got a plan? You've always got a plan."

"Here, Dug old lad, have a squint at these messages," Max handed his phone to Duggie.

"See, we aren't alone, Dug, we've got people behind us, looking out for us, covering our backs. I guess we'll recover, go back to work and carry on until the next episode hits us."

"Yep, sounds about right to me. It looks like you'll have the long arms of the law wrapped around you too," said Duggie, happy for his friend, happy for himself.

Also by Anthony Silman

A frenzied drug pusher brutally attacks Jo Hadge on her doorstep late at night. Terrified, she defends herself and, in desperate danger, lashes out and stabs him.

But it is Jo who ends up in court and must face a tense, nerve-shredding trial.

Dan, her partner and lover, believes in her innocence. He wants revenge. He creates a devastating sham social media campaign of retribution, posting fictitious deepfake videos of character destruction.

A horrifying international cataclysm follows his brilliant comeuppance. From the UK to Ohio to Mexico and Ecuador, Dan's crusade wreaks terrible repercussions on the families and gangs of cocaine suppliers.

Suddenly a psychopathic IT mogul, a cartel boss, dealers and pushers are all caught by Dan's deepfake sting – but who will pay, and what is the shocking price of a lover's vengeance?

About the Author

Anthony (Tony) Silman has been writing for most of his life, as a newspaper columnist and editor as well as script, copy and speech writing for global company programmes, conferences, press and product launches and major events.

His fact-finding and research instincts, combined with his fascination with emerging technologies and the effects of new digital media on today's and future society, create the essence of his books which, although fictional, have a core of facts and real-life occurrences.

Max Bomber Revenge is his second book in the 'Max' series. It involves hacking, trolling, and state-sponsored misinformation. Addiction, rehabilitation, drug-pushing, violence, and sex traps also feature in this story of courage, survival and unusual justice.

Tony lives in Wiltshire, UK with his beloved wife, Sarah.

*Available worldwide from Amazon
and all good bookstores*

Michael Terence Publishing

www.mtp.agency

www.facebook.com/mtp.agency

@mtp_agency

www.ingramcontent.com/pod-product-compliance
Lightning Source LLC
LaVergne TN
LVHW041631060526
838200LV00040B/1534